CIRQUE

BROOKLYNN LANGSTON

Printed in the United States of America

2020 First Edition

10 9 8 7 6 5 4 3 2 1

Subject Index:

Langston, Brooklynn

Title: Cirque

1. Teen & Young Adult Fiction 2. Teen & Young Adult Social Issues 3. Teen & Young Adult Mystery & Suspense 4. Hopelessness 5. Self-Harm 6. Suicidal Thoughts 7. Physical Abuse 8. Bullying

Illustration Credit: All chapter illustrations were created by Bim Flores - instagram: @bimbostix

Paperback ISBN: 978-1-7343273-0-4

Library of Congress Card Catalog Number: 2019919261

Langston Publishing LLC

ourcirque.com

WELCOME TO CIRQUE...

For You.

This book is for anyone who has ever felt scared, alone, not good enough, not smart enough, or unwanted. Anyone who has ever wished they'd never been born. Anyone who has ever been abused, raped, bullied, or targeted.

This story is for every boy and girl who knelt over a toilet bowl in an attempt to became valuable. For every boy and girl who grew up watching their parents fade away with drugs, alcohol, and violence. For anyone who ever felt like they had no idea who they were.

Anyone who felt like they didn't belong in their own family. Anyone who ever wondered if they were special. Anyone who ever wondered if they were meant for something big. Anyone who ever wanted to change the world.

Grab a pen or a highlighter. Underline or circle anything that speaks to you. Anything that moves you. Write your thoughts in the margins. And when you have experienced Cirque and all it has to offer, find someone else who needs it.

None of us are alone.

B Forest

TABLE OF CONTENTS

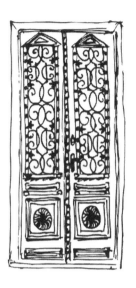

PART 1

CHAPTER 1. DREW

A horrible pain shot through the back of Drew's head as it made contact with the cold metal high school locker. Two boys with nothing better to do, stood in front of him mocking, laughing, and ruining any hopes he had of a peaceful day.

"Fag."

"Homo."

Each shot a word but neither of them realized the amount of irreparable damage that was being done to Drew. He gulped down the lump in his throat and tried to stand tall, but no matter how high he lifted his head, he was being looked down upon by morons who thought they were better. He was being ridiculed for something he had no control over. He closed his eyes and tried to find a happy thought to hide in. He wanted to think of his parents, but their presence in his mind was tainted.

Drew then thought of his room, of his computer and the online games that he lost himself in trying to feel a sense of purpose. He found confidence in winning battles in the digital world but was too scared to fight back in the real one.

Plenty of other students casually passed through the hallway while all of this was happening. Most didn't even realize what was going on, the few who did averted their eyes and ignored the painful reality. *Cowards!* Drew screamed in his head. *Why won't anyone help me? Why won't at least one person stand up and defend me?*

You're such a hypocrite, the voice in Drew's head whispered to him. *Why don't you stand up and defend yourself? Here you are wanting others to have courage when you don't even have an ounce of it.* Drew knew that voice was right. *Who am I to talk about having guts? I'm a coward, the biggest one.*

The bell rang, the taunting finally ceased, and Drew was left with their words and laughter on repeat in his mind. He gripped the straps of his backpack and his stomach twisted with nerves as he walked to his geometry class. He dreaded the rest of the day ahead of him.

Today was going to be like every other day. He would sit in class, ignore everyone and everything, and plan his escape. He would do his schoolwork quickly and quietly, trying to concentrate and do it correctly. He would tap his foot on the floor or his fingers on the desk, anticipating for each class period to be over.

He swore to himself that one of these days he would have the nerve to run away and never look back. Who needed school anyway? Plenty of people made a good living without high school. He could just go back for his GED or something. He didn't need this day-to-day torture.

But every morning he woke up, got dressed, and went to school anyway. He could never run away. He wouldn't have the first clue what to do once he got out on his own. It wouldn't be a full twenty-four hours before he was crawling home into his room and settling back into the horrible routine that was his life. He felt trapped, locked in a cycle that was suffocating him, waiting for the day it would end.

Drew stood with his lunch tray in hand, waiting to receive what everyone in the school considered non-food. The cafeteria was filled with four hundred students laughing, arguing, quizzing each other and copying homework. Drew wished more than anything that he could blend into the noise and the normalcy that came with it.

He moved along the line and handed his tray to the lunch man who tossed what looked like a hamburger on his plate. Next to him, two guys were talking in vivid detail about their weekend. He tried to mind his own business but he couldn't help but overhear them boast about the girls they had been with. Drew felt anger start to bubble up inside of him. *Why can't I be like that?* he thought. *Why can't I be normal? Why do I have to be the only one to feel like this?*

Drew quickly paid for his meal and sat at the end of the long table in the corner of the lunchroom. A few other people sat near him but no one talked to each other. Everyone had headphones on or books in front of them. He picked at his food, he hadn't had much of an appetite lately. He pulled out his phone and played games on it for the rest of the lunch period.

Every time he walked down the hallway, Drew's insecurities put him on high alert. He felt like everyone was judging him or laughing at him. The students, the teachers—there was nowhere he could go to get away from them. He wanted to disappear, he wanted to stay in bed forever. Every day he woke up feeling worse than the day before. Home was hell, school was hell— there was no peace. He walked into his history classroom and quickly went to his seat.

The classroom chatter continued until the bell rang. He felt jealousy rise up inside of him as he watched his classmates laugh with each other. Maybe if he wasn't so quiet he would have friends. *No,* he corrected himself. *They would reject me if I put myself out there. It's easier to be alone.*

He looked out of the classroom window and peered at the sidewalk two floors down. He imagined himself standing on the ledge of the roof, trying to decide whether or not to jump. He'd thought about it hundreds of times, it'd be so easy. All he had to do was close his eyes, take a deep breath, and fall. All his classmates would notice him then.

They would notice when his broken body was splattered on the sidewalk. Maybe they would feel bad. Maybe they would regret every horrible word they had directed at him. All those times they had harassed him would come back to haunt every single one of them forever. They would have weighing guilt on their conscience.

They all deserve that, Drew thought to himself.

"Drew!" He was pulled back to reality by the voice of his history teacher. "Pay attention." He nodded his head and his teacher continued writing notes on the board.

"Busy replaying a gay porno in your head?" a voice whispered from the desk behind him.

Drew clenched his jaw shut in an attempt to contain a few choice words that he was aching to scream out at the top of his lungs. The number one reason he hated this class was because of the person sitting behind him. Ben would always have something to say as if he spent his whole day thinking up the insults.

Ben continued, "What would your mother think? Are you too scared to tell her? I think you should. She deserves to know her son has wandering eyes in the locker room."

"That's not true," Drew said quietly.

Ben laughed. "Oh please, princess. Everyone knows you stare."

Drew opened his mouth to defend himself but realized it would do no good. They would always have the last word. They would always beat him, always overpower him.

Drew could hear snickering behind him as the sound of his teacher talking continued. He gripped the edge of his desk as it was pushed forward. He didn't have to look to know Ben had kicked it.

Drew couldn't wait to lock himself in his room. He loved the short while of isolation he had before he would have to come back and do this all over again. The school bell had never sounded so sweet to a student's ears than it did that afternoon to his.

He didn't even bother going to his locker. He walked right out the front door and put his headphones on. He tried to imagine what life would be like after high school. He would have to go to college. He wondered if people were as mean in college as they were in high school. He would have to pick a career path. He would have to talk to people and go on interviews and try to make something of himself.

A thought entered his mind, the idea of working with computers. He had considered it before, he had thought about it a lot actually. He could create websites, he could do coding, he could even design video games—that would be amazing.

Anxiety crept up his throat. He wouldn't be able to do any of that stuff. He could barely hold a conversation with his mother, let alone a stranger. Not to mention he could already hear his father laughing and insulting the desire to work with computers. What was he going to do with his life? He certainly wasn't going to stay with his parents. Where would he end up then? He would become a nobody. Another empty face in a crowd, a name that would never be remembered.

"Hi, sweetie." Drew closed his front door behind him. Anna took a break from seasoning a chicken that would go to waste that night and gave her son a kiss on the cheek. "How was school?" she asked.

"Good." The lie slipped past his lips as easily as he slipped off his jacket. He didn't even consider telling his mom about the slight concussion he possibly received and the suicidal thoughts that never stopped running through his mind.

Drew walked into the kitchen and grabbed a water from the fridge. His mother continued to talk to him, but he wasn't even pretending to listen. He was thinking of all the clever comebacks he could've used today if he hadn't been such a wuss.

"Hey, you two." Drew's dad came into the kitchen, unclipped his name tag and set it on the table. Drew observed the tag and took notice of how the "F" in Frank was slightly bigger than the other letters.

"Got plans tonight, kid?" Frank asked. He grabbed a beer from the fridge.

"No," Drew replied.

"No hot date?" His dad smiled slyly. He seemed to enjoy mocking his one and only child, claiming that it was loving teasing. Drew never felt the love in anything his father said or did. He rolled his eyes at the comment and started up the stairs.

"Where are you going?" Frank asked.

"My room."

"You're just gonna play on your computer all night?" Frank asked with annoyance.

Drew responded by closing his bedroom door loud enough to be heard but not loud enough to be classified as a slam, which would then lead to confrontation with Frank and that was the last thing Drew wanted. He was scared of the bullies at school, sure, but he was even more terrified of the bully that lived down the hall.

Drew clicked the mouse harshly and a headache was starting to form as he clenched his teeth and leaned too close to the computer. He sighed and paused his game. He could hear the sound of his father's voice from downstairs and it made his blood boil. He hated his dad, there was no doubt about it. Drew laid down on his bed and stared at the ceiling. For as long as he could remember he had been at odds with his father.

In Frank's eyes, Drew never did anything right, neither did his mom, no matter how hard they tried, and they really did try. His mother even started seeing a therapist. Drew refused to go when she suggested he join her. All the therapist did was prescribe anti-anxiety meds, which his mother now swore by. In his opinion, all the pills did was make her even more compliant with whatever his father said.

Drew looked over at the few small trophies on his dresser. Baseball, soccer, and basketball. He only played when he was younger because Frank dragged him to the games and practices. He hated playing sports, mostly because of how his father would act if he didn't do well, which was the majority of the time. Drew just wasn't into it. He hated standing in the beaming sun, he hated the pressure, and he hated how he wasn't as good as the other guys on the team. His father would yell and curse and lecture Drew, and tell him that he wouldn't get far in life if he couldn't even kick a soccer ball correctly.

He rolled over with his face in his pillow.

From his room, he could smell dinner and his stomach grumbled, longing for something to fill it. He began to make his way downstairs but stopped when he got to the top of the staircase.

"I just don't understand, Anna! What's the matter with him? Where did we go wrong?" Drew's stomach dropped when he heard those words come out of his father's mouth. From so many years of eavesdropping, his parents had hundreds of conversations about Drew that they didn't know he heard, most of which Drew wished he hadn't heard.

"There's nothing wrong with him. It's just a phase," Anna said.

A phase. That's what he tried to make himself believe. He tried to assure himself that life wouldn't be this difficult forever, that he would be normal someday and people would stop treating him so badly. He was in the sixth grade when he told himself that, and as far as Drew could tell, things weren't ever going to change. If anything, they were just going to get worse.

"It's not a phase. It's who he's letting himself be. He sits on his damn computer all day and night, he has no friends, and he isolates himself. He's a queer, too, for God's sake!"

"Frank!" Anna yelled in bewilderment.

Drew clenched his fists and tried to fight the tears that were threatening to fall.

"He needs to be handled. That life might be acceptable for other people but not me, not my son!"

"He's just going through a rough patch. He has a tough time at school. Kids these days are cruel," Anna responded. *Cruel is an understatement,* Drew thought.

"Kids were cruel when I was growing up, too. If he would toughen up he wouldn't get knocked around so much," Frank said.

Yeah, that'll help, Drew defended in his mind. *If I try to stand up for myself I'll only get hit harder.*

"You need to be more understanding," Anna countered.

"He needs to be more of a man!" Frank yelled.

Drew couldn't handle it anymore, his voice overpowered his father's as he flew down the stairs, "Don't tell me to be a man, you hypocrite!"

"You watch your mouth, boy!" his father yelled back.

"No!" Drew took a step forward. "If anyone's a coward it's you! You're scared of anything that's different and anything that doesn't go your way!"

"Shut up! Go back and play your stupid little game!"

"Frank!" Anna cried.

"Enough, Anna! We've babied him for too damn long and look what happened. It's time for him to grow the hell up!" Frank poked his finger into Drew's chest roughly.

"I hate you!" Drew screamed and swatted his father's hand away from him. He sprinted upstairs to his bathroom and locked the door.

He could still hear his father yelling from downstairs and his mother trying to calm him down. Frank was no doubt trying to come upstairs and continue the fight. It wouldn't be the first time.

Drew slid onto the floor, letting the tears fall freely. He was done. He couldn't do this anymore. There was no point. This had been going on for too long. He had cried on this bathroom floor one too many times. He looked up at the medicine cabinet. He had considered it hundreds of times, even back in middle school. He looked down at the floor.

"Don't you dare take his side, Anna. This is your fault!" Frank screamed.

Drew looked back at the medicine cabinet. He hiccuped and shakily stood. He looked at himself in the mirror. He averted his eyes. More tears fell onto his hands as they gripped the sink. He looked back up at the mirror. The whole day flashed before his eyes, and then the past several years. He hiccuped again trying to stop crying. He turned the small gold knob on the cabinet and opened it quickly so as not to keep looking at himself.

He sat back down again. The bathroom was silent apart from Drew's heavy breathing. He turned the little orange bottle around in his hands. The sound of his mother's pills rattling made everything more real. Thoughts were racing through his mind at a hundred miles an hour. He thought of every day he ever took a beating for being "different." He thought about every name he had been called. He thought about every time he felt non-existent, every time he felt like no one would even care if he disappeared, every disapproving look his father gave him— every time he felt irrelevant.

He thought about what it would be like if he continued going to school. He thought about all the abuse he had yet to receive. All the jokes and hurtful words that had yet to be aimed at him. He thought about what the rest of his life would be like if every day was going to be like today. He wouldn't be able to handle it.

As he went deeper and deeper into his mind, the pills looked more and more desirable. He tried to blink away the blurriness in his eyes. He steadied his breathing and twisted off the bottle cap. *I have to,* he told himself. *I can't do this anymore.*

With those thoughts Drew popped the pills into his mouth and swallowed them down.

CHAPTER 2. RECRUITMENT

The man with the top hat sat on the floor of the bathroom. Drew was slumped against the wall across from him. The man pleaded with Drew to stop. He begged him to close the cap and put the bottle away, but his voice went unheard. Drew decided his fate. His breathing was haggard and his eyelids were heavy. Tears continued to flow and his chest continued to heave.

"Oh, Drew," the man sighed.

He wiped his own tears and then reached over to wipe Drew's. Drew's eyes were completely shut now and his breathing would stop at any moment. The voices of Anna and Frank grew increasingly louder as they continued to yell at each other, not thinking about consoling their son. They were so oblivious. The man with the top hat shook his head in anger.

"Don't worry, Drew," he whispered. "It's going to be okay. Your life is not over, this is not your end." The man swung Drew's arm around his shoulders and lifted him up. He tapped his black cane on the floor twice.

All that was left in the bathroom was a cloud of glittery red smoke.

CHAPTER 3. LILLY

She wiped her lips with the back of her hand and grabbed the counter above her as she stood. The room began to spin, causing Lilly to close her eyes and take a deep breath. After doing this so many times, she felt she had mastered the side effects of purging. Feeling that the world was steady, Lilly opened her eyes and relaxed.

The music playing from her room floated into the bathroom. She flushed the toilet and then vigorously brushed her teeth, trying to rid the taste of spaghetti from her mouth. Staring into the mirror, she cringed at the girl staring back. She put the finishing touches on her makeup. A dark lipstick, lots of mascara, and some glitter here and there. Looking in the mirror, all Lilly could see was fatness even as she stroked her protruding collarbone.

"Why can't I just be thin?" she whispered.

Lilly looked at her phone and saw it was a quarter to ten—almost time.

"Goodnight, mom!" She called from the second floor down to the first.

"Night, sweetie!" She could tell from her mom's tone that she was immersed in paperwork. Her little sister was fast asleep and so was her dad since he had to be up before daybreak for an early shift.

With something too short and too tight clinging to her fragile frame, Lilly opened her window and climbed down the side of her house. She attempted to hang onto the ivy and the old wooden ladder that it clung to. Her mother loved to garden, they used to work in the yard together. Lilly stopped climbing for a moment. It seemed like so long ago that she was digging into the ground, laughing at a story from her mother's childhood. So long ago when her heart was light and she had no worries.

"Do you want me to teach you how I stay skinny?" Lilly nodded at her bunkmate as they sat in their cabin at a soccer camp. She followed her friend into the bathroom and her stomach twisted in a knot when she saw her stick her fingers down her throat.

Lilly backed away. "No, never mind. I would never do that."

The girl flushed the toilet and washed her hands. She rolled her eyes at Lilly and said, "You're being dramatic, but whatever. Not everyone is cut out for it, I guess." The girl pushed past Lilly and left the cabin.

Headlights passing by caught Lilly's attention and she continued her descent. Once her bare feet hit the ground, she put on her shoes. Her heels click-clacked on the sidewalk as she neared the familiar piece of junk car owned by her best friend.

"Took ya' long enough," Maria spoke through the open passenger window.

Lilly grasped the door handle to open it and ended up pulling it completely off. "I hate this car!" she groaned. Maria laughed as Lilly strategically maneuvered the handle back in place and this time opened the door with great caution.

An overplayed pop song filled the car as the girls drove to the party that had their whole school talking. Lilly's fingers drummed nervously on her thigh whereas Maria was oozing confidence. It was always like that. Maria didn't have to try to be loved by everyone. Lilly had to work hard to be noticed and even harder to remain that way, all while also trying to get her weight down—it was exhausting.

The two of them had become friends freshman year as they braved the world of high school volleyball, stressful math classes and awkward moments in the cafeteria. Maria had a little bit of an idea about Lilly's complicated relationship with food. They had both been trying every diet out there, but Maria had no clue what lengths her friend was going to in order to stay thin. Lilly worked hard keeping it from everyone close to her.

"So you're still grounded? That's why you went all Tarzan getting out the house?" Maria asked. Lilly laughed with her friend.

"Yeah, my mom was pissed when I came home drunk. And for the fact that I puked all over the couch." Lilly was embarrassed just thinking about it.

Her parents had been devastated. She had never gotten into any kind of trouble before, she was their perfect child. Perfect grades, perfect behavior, perfect attitude, but that night she had gone too far. She clenched her fist and her nails dug into her skin as she thought about it.

"Gross!" Maria exclaimed.

"Yeah, so for the next three weekends I'm supposed to be trapped in the house thinking about the consequences of underage drinking and the path of life that it's leading me down," Lilly said in a mocking tone.

"Blah, blah, blah." Maria giggled. Lilly laughed along and stared out of the window.

After a moment she asked her friend, "Did you get your results back yet?"

Maria's carefree face shifted into one of stress. Her voice was low, "No. Not yet."

They both got lost in the memory of the cold white-walled clinic they were in a few days ago. Lilly had sat in the stuffy waiting room while Maria got tested. HIV came back negative, but they were waiting to hear about the others.

Maria visibly shook off her bummed out attitude and put on a smile. "But never mind that! Tonight we're having fun. No need to worry, so stop thinking about it." Lilly nodded. Maria turned the music up and they both sang along.

Within a few minutes, the car was parked at the curb and the pair of high schoolers were linked arm in arm walking up to the front door. The music was already too loud without them even being inside. When the door opened and a drunken welcome was shouted, but barely heard, Lilly put on her fake smile and false air of self-security and joined the party.

"I'll go get drinks!" Maria shouted. Lilly nodded her head in response. She watched as Maria made her way through the crowd, being hit on and envied by people she passed.

Lilly sighed, no one ever looked at her like that. She was nothing special, no matter how hard she worked at it. She waved to a couple of girls on her volleyball team, and a guy from her AP bio class, while Maria walked back and handed Lilly a cup.

"You're driving." Lilly put the cup to her lips after reminding her friend.

Maria rolled her eyes. "Beer hardly does anything to me. I'm only gonna have one or two, we'll be fine. It's only like a five-minute ride." Lilly gave her an unconvinced look.

"Come on!" Maria grabbed Lilly's hand and dragged her into the crowd. After emptying her cup and dancing with people she didn't even know, Lilly realized that she had been separated from Maria. She gathered her bearings and managed to break through the crowd and end up on the back porch. Smoke immediately attacked her, as did a fit of coughs. Once she could breathe again she noticed the group passing around a blunt. One guy offered it to her, but she shook her head no.

She searched for something other than smoking to distract her. She spotted Maria in the middle of a group of basketball players. Lilly put her arm around her friend, earning a giggle from Maria and the attention of the group.

"Guys, this is my best friend Lilly. Lilly, these are my new friends." Maria took a sip of whatever was in her cup and smiled a gorgeous smile.

"Hi," Lilly said, smiling shyly at one of the guys she caught staring at her. Maria broke away from Lilly's grasp and was willingly guided to a secluded corner, wrapping her arms around some guy's neck.

"So, Lilly, I'm Damian." The staring stranger took a step forward and placed his hand on her hip. "Let me get you another drink." She blushed and nodded.

Not too long after, Lilly's head was spinning. Her body moved wherever Damian's hands moved it. He kissed her neck and she knew where this night would end, just like it had with another boy for the first time at the beginning of the summer. She stopped thinking about that and kissed Damian back.

She followed close behind as he led her upstairs, down the hall, and into a bedroom. She kissed him as he laid her on the bed. She was okay with this. She wanted this. She was supposed to do this. This is what happened at parties. This was normal.

He thought she was pretty so he wanted her. He thought she was worthy enough to be touched. She craved the affection he would give her, even though it would only be for a short time. Doing this made her feel important. He liked her because she was skinny. He liked her because of her makeup and her clothes. He liked her for everything she did to be like everybody else. All her hard work was paying off.

Afterward, he stood up and slid his shirt back on. Before Lilly could say a word Damian had closed the door behind him. He hadn't even looked at her, his eyes were on her yes, but he didn't truly see her. She sat on the edge of the bed and did everything in her power to shut off her mind. She didn't want to face the truth. But sitting there alone in that dark bedroom, Lilly couldn't run away from it. She knew better.

She knew that stupid boy didn't like her. She knew he only wanted her for sex. That's all they ever wanted. She was only good for one thing. She wasn't smart enough to be loved for her brain. She wasn't funny enough to be loved for her humor. She wasn't talented enough to be loved for her accomplishments. She was barely pretty enough to be loved for her body. That's why it was always dark. They didn't want to see her. She didn't even want to see herself.

"Don't even think about it, Lilly. He wouldn't go for you." The girls once again sat on their beds as they discussed the boys at their camp. A few more girls had joined the conversation this time. Lilly clenched her fist causing her nails to go into her skin. The habit had begun the past school year during her sports seasons. The stress and anxiety needing some sort of release.

"Why not?" Lilly asked. She thought she was pretty. Her parents had always told her she was. Why wouldn't the boy like her?

"He likes fit girls. Skinny girls. You're just not there yet. He won't want to date you. He already likes me." Again, Lilly's fists tightened.

She raised her chin and tried her very hardest not to cry. The other girls giggled and moved onto another topic, but her heart was breaking, her mind reeling with confusion.

Lilly wiped her tears away and stood up. She found a bathroom and fixed her makeup as best she could after having too many drinks. She stepped uneasily down the stairs and back into the party. She stood amongst the crowd, a hundred teenagers packed in tight. She felt empty. There was a pit in her stomach. She felt alone, completely alone. She felt invisible.

She was still a little buzzed, but she knew that she was starting to get dizzy for a different reason. She looked for Maria but her friend was nowhere to be found. Lilly felt her stomach churn and she knew she had to get out of that house. She meekly pushed her way through the crowd to the door. Once outside, she made it as far as the curb before throwing up.

She lost count of how long she had been doubled over puking her brains out. Everything was in fours wherever she looked. It took twice as long as it should've for her to walk home. Once she did, it took about three tries to get up and through the window—it was a miracle she did at all. When she finally made into her room, she knocked into her dresser causing a family photo to fall to her feet. She picked it up and her eyes tried to focus.

The photo had been taken two years ago, the summer before freshman year. Her father had just gotten a promotion so he decided to treat the family to an expensive dinner. She remembered stuffing her face gladly. She shuddered at the memory.

"Are you going to go back next year?" Lilly's mother asked. The four of them sat in a restaurant celebrating. Her mom was talking about soccer camp, Lilly shook her head. "Why not?" her mom asked.

Lilly just shrugged as she shoved another forkful in her mouth.

"Slow down there kid, don't want you to swell up like a balloon." Her dad chuckled innocently. Her mother laughed and shoved his arm. Her little sister mimicked a balloon blowing up and then popping.

That night Lilly sat in her bathroom cross-legged in front of the toilet. She fiddled with her hands replaying the summer in her mind. Replaying the mean words, the rejection, the comments from her family that they didn't even realize held so much power.

She cried as she leaned over the toilet. She cried while she threw up her dad's celebratory dinner, she cried while she brushed her teeth and washed her hands, she cried as she got into bed, and she cried until she fell asleep.

Lilly put the picture back in its place and began prying off the clothes that suffocated her, replacing them with ones three sizes too big, making her feel smaller. Coming out of her closet she clung to the door frame as her legs shook. She made it to her bed but couldn't find the will to even get under the covers. Her chest hurt as bad as her head did.

She imagined being anywhere else other than in her bedroom, feeling like this. She imagined being on a beach. Feeling the breeze and the sand, being completely carefree. Not obsessing over what she looked like in a swimsuit, not being mindful about covering herself up with a towel. She fell asleep imagining the ocean.

Lilly woke up the next morning feeling worse than she had in a long time. She forced herself out of bed. She put on her running clothes and drank some water before setting out on her usual morning run. She pushed her body harder even when it screamed at her to stop. The volleyball championship was coming up and she had to be in her best shape. Her muscles were begging her to quit, her stomach was calling out for her to eat something, anything, and keep it down. She took deep breaths and kept running.

The house was quiet when she returned, everyone was taking advantage of the ability to sleep in on Saturday morning. Lilly slipped off her shoes and grabbed ahold of the wall during a dizzy spell. She felt her stomach twist and turn and she bent over. Her arm felt funny and she clutched at her chest. She slid down to the ground and leaned against the front door trying to catch her breath.

She looked up at the ceiling, she clenched and unclenched her fists. She saw spots in her vision and was suddenly so light-headed she swore she would float away any second. She could hear distant footsteps, someone was coming down the stairs. She opened her mouth to speak but nothing came out. *What's happening? What's wrong with me? Why does my chest hurt?*

She thought about how her family would find her like this. They would blame themselves. They would wonder why none of them noticed Lilly deteriorating. They would wonder where they went wrong, why did their daughter feel this way? They would be racked with guilt and pain. Maria would be so confused and would probably blame herself, too. Her coaches and teachers would be disappointed. She had let everyone down.

Darkness started creeping in from the corner of her eyes.

She clenched and unclenched her fists.

Her heart sped up and knocked horribly in her chest.

She slumped even lower on the ground until she heard her heart no more.

CHAPTER 4. RECRUITMENT

The man with the top hat stood beside Lilly as she threw up. He could hear the voices of intoxicated teenagers and his stomach twisted at the thought of all those poor kids just looking for something to fill the empty spots. Lilly continued to vomit and he rubbed her back, she showed no signs that she knew he was there. Finally, she stood up straight, stumbled a bit, and began walking home.

She held her shoes in her hands and he did his best to guide her home. It was hard to do since she had no clue he was walking beside her. Eventually, they were in front of her house and he tried to get her to go through the front door so her mother could take care of her, but she was determined to climb back up to her room.

The man with the top hat helped her keep her balance and when she couldn't get the window open, he opened it for her and got her safely inside.

"Lilly," he called out to her after she ran into her dresser.

She couldn't hear him. He had hoped that her drunken state would have at least opened her mind a bit, but she was still so lost in her own thoughts. His heart broke for her as she looked at her family photo with such sad, tired eyes.

"Lilly," he tried one more time after she came out of her closet. She collapsed on her bed. He put a blanket over her and she fell asleep.

The next morning, after a run she shouldn't have pushed herself to do, she shook as she fell to the floor clutching at her chest. The man with the top hat heard footsteps coming down the stairs. He wrapped his arms around Lilly and with two taps of a cane echoing on the hardwood floor, they disappeared.

CHAPTER 5. JORDAN

Sirens echoed as Jordan sat in an alleyway. He brought his hand up to his mouth and took a hit—inhale, exhale—as he stared at the brick wall across from him, at the dumpster and at the graffiti. He inhaled again and thought back to earlier in the day.

"Jordan, are you even listening to me?!" Roger Blight, a seasoned parole officer, raised his voice at the seventeen-year-old delinquent that sat slouched in a faded beige armchair with a hole in the seat cushion. Jordan seemed aloof to the fact that he was in deep trouble for violating his probation.

"No, sir," Jordan responded. The officer sighed and pinched the bridge of his nose in an attempt to contain his temper.

"Do you not understand that you're reaching the end of your rope? One more week and you'll be eighteen—"

"Week and two days actually," Jordan interrupted.

Officer Blight continued after giving Jordan the most annoyed look he could muster, "Being eighteen means no more

Juvi, no more slack, no more easy way out. I can't keep giving you warnings and community service hours. The Judge is going to want more severe actions. It's time for you to get serious."

Jordan broke the lead point off a pencil he had taken from Blight's desk.

"Jordan. I get it, okay? You're tough. You're a brick wall and all that crap, but your future is something to care about. Show some emotion, kid," Blight pleaded. He leaned against his desk.

Jordan's face was painted with his usual solemn look. *Be a man. Men don't cry.* His father's words echoed through Jordan's thoughts as images vividly started to flood his mind. His eight-year-old self was standing small and insignificant in the living room staring into the fire that manifested in his father's eyes. Little Jordan's cheek stung and his eyes watered as he stared at the back of his father's hand.

Jordan had come home upset, he had run all the way from school. Some bigger kids in his class had pushed him down and kicked him a few times. Jordan didn't even know why he was getting beat up, all he knew was that it hurt. He got away as fast as he could and sobbed the entire fifteen-minute commute back home.

He never cried in front of his father again after that day. Instead, he hid in his room, or ran away, or screamed into his pillow, or hit something—anything to keep from crying. He would do anything to avoid the disgusted look and bruised face he had gotten from his father.

"Jordan," Blight's exasperated voice snapped Jordan out of his memory and caused him to lock eyes with the one man that genuinely cared about his well-being. "Look," Blight leaned forward, trying desperately to get Jordan to hear the words coming out of his mouth. "Despite what you and everyone else thinks, I believe—I truly believe that you have the potential to do great things. You could get out of this God-forsaken city and do something with your life."

Jordan's eyebrows creased in confusion. "There's no way in hell I'm getting out of here. I'm trapped—chains and all."

"You don't have to be," Blight countered, but Jordan shook his stubborn head.

"I'll lay low. See ya'." Jordan saluted the irritated, underpaid officer, placed the broken pencil on the desk, and left.

Jordan's hands rested in his jacket pockets as he sauntered down the dirty sidewalks of his neighborhood. He stared intently at the ground in front of him as he did every day, taking in every detail about the polluted, meaningless concrete. He memorized the cracks and the stains and knew exactly where one part of the cement would rise higher than the other due to the carelessness of a construction worker. Jordan could make it home completely blind needing no assistance whatsoever, all the way up to the front, dangerously loose, uneven steps of his apartment building.

He sympathized with the sidewalk. Just like Jordan, the sidewalk was a small factor in everyday life that was always being mindlessly overlooked. Just like Jordan, it had its imperfections and mistakes, and they would always show. No matter how much time had passed, they would always remain. And just like Jordan, the cement that was poured and paved so long ago, was trapped in this doomed city. Never changing, never improving and never ever escaping.

He closed the door to apartment 331 behind him and went straight to the kitchen. He pulled out the container of leftover Chinese and put it in the microwave. He looked in the fridge for something else to fill him up, but all he saw was half a bottle of flat Sprite and a stick of butter. His stomach growled and he slammed the fridge door shut, causing a few empty cereal boxes to topple down onto the eggshell-white kitchen tiles.

The microwave dinged and he ate the little fried rice and chicken before it even cooled off. He drank from the kitchen faucet and wiped his mouth with his sleeve. The door to his parents' bedroom opened and his mom stepped out.

"Hey, J." She smiled at him while pulling at the sleeves of her shirt. "Where you been?"

"Just out." He could tell by her drooping eyes that she was high. It was rare to see her sober anymore. It had been almost a whole year of her being clean. A year of peace, of food in the house, of laughter and good times—and then he came back home.

"Sarah!" It's a sad sight when a mother and a son both flinch at the sound of a father's voice, but that was a regular occurrence all throughout Jordan's life. It was the only reaction he had ever known to have towards his father. "Brian's at the door. I need the money."

Some drunkards are clumsy and sloppy, and sometimes quite funny to watch, not Jordan's father though. His words were as firm drunk as they were sober, and his eyes were just as dangerous. Looking at him, Jordan decided his dad didn't deserve the name, Gabriel. Gabriel was too gentle sounding, it didn't fit his harsh nature.

"I'll get it. It's in the room," Sarah's shoulders were tense as she spoke. Her eyes were cautious as she watched the unpredictable man and her fingers slightly shook at the thought of what he was capable of.

Seeing his mother so vulnerable made Jordan want to get her as far away from Gabriel as possible; she would never leave him though. "I love him, J," she would tell him, "He wasn't always like this, he's just going through a hard time." Till her last breath, she would defend Gabriel, even though he was the last person on earth that deserved it.

Gabriel let out a grunt of approval and headed to the apartment door. Sarah didn't meet Jordan's eyes. He watched her go into her room, reach under the bed, and get out her savings money. She liked to say she was saving up for a better home or for a sunny vacation, but really all she was saving up for was money to give their dealer.

Jordan heard Brian's disgusting voice come from the hallway. It took everything in him not to go and slam the door in his face. Jordan had learned his lesson long ago to never get in the way of a deal. He had tried, several times, to keep his mom from getting high. He had flushed it down the toilet, hidden it in his own room, thrown it out the window into the alley, and every single time he would get the beating of a lifetime from his dad. Even Sarah would yell angry words at him. He had given up stopping them when he was twelve.

Sarah walked through the living room and handed a wad of cash to Brian. Brian handed Gabriel a baggie and shouted an unreciprocated hello to Jordan. Gabriel went into his bedroom without looking at his son.

"I love you, J." Sarah gave him a weak hug.

"I love you, too, ma'." He wrapped his arm loosely around her. She patted his back and then went into her room.

He stared at the closed bedroom door for a minute, letting himself imagine what life could be if his father was gone and his mother was clean. It made him sad, which made him angry. He slammed the apartment door on his way out.

Jordan didn't plan on staying home that night. He walked to the bus stop two blocks from his house, got on without paying, and sat in the very back. The fluorescent lighting made everyone look miserable. Jordan just looked down at his hands not wanting to look at the window and see his reflection. Ten minutes later he pressed the bar above him and the driver slowed down at his stop.

"Hey!" Will sat on the stoop of his apartment building on his phone. He and Jordan had been in the same class all throughout school. They were neighbors for a long time until Will's dad went to jail and he moved in with his mom and her boyfriend.

The boys walked down the block together to the only place that would let them in. They sat at the bar and ordered two drinks from Ali, their favorite bartender. She knew they were underage but she didn't care. She was only a couple years older but always had a thing for Jordan, he figured a hook up every once in a while was worth a seat at the bar.

"How was Blight today?" Will asked before taking a sip of his beer.

"Same as always," Jordan told him, as he picked up the first of many shots set out before him. Ali had been generous with drinks today. "Telling me I need to get my act together before I get thrown in jail. How did it go for you today? The interview?"

"Good, I got the job. Right there on the spot." Will smiled proudly. He had been trying to clean up his act and it finally paid off.

"Now that's something to toast to. Ali." Ali came over and the three of them toasted with a shot.

"What's the job?" she asked.

"Just customer service but I can work my way up in the company to a manager and then whatever comes after that." Ali giggled as she poured the guys another drink.

"I always wanted to start my own business," she told them.

"What happened?" Will asked her. Jordan couldn't have cared less, he just wanted more to drink.

"Didn't have enough money to stay in school—I couldn't keep taking out loans. I figured out I was good at bartending and that's that." She shrugged, trying to play off her disappointment. She turned away as a group called for refills.

The boys were silent for a while. A football game was on in the background, low music played from the other room in the bar. Pool balls knocked against the sides of the billiard table. Drunken conversations and the sounds of glasses being set on the bar echoed. It was a mundane night, but Will was sick of the mundane.

"He's right ya' know," Will said quietly while peeling the label off his bottle.

"What?" Jordan didn't take his eyes off the TV screen.

"Blight's right, 'bout getting your act together and stuff."

"Whatever."

"You don't need to end up in prison." Jordan looked at his friend after he said that.

"You've had a job less than a day. Don't try and act better than me—trying to tell me what to do," Jordan told him. Will rolled his eyes.

"I'm not saying I'm better and I'm not trying to tell you what to do. I'm just saying you don't need to throw your life away," Will said.

"There's nothing about my life to throw away. I'll eventually end up in prison anyway so why not get a head start?" Jordan smiled cynically. The shot glass was cold against his lips.

"Shut up, man. You can achieve stuff, set goals and things like that."

"I don't have goals." Jordan's throat burned slightly, but it didn't stop him from raising another shot.

"Yeah, you do, you just won't admit to yourself cause you don't want to be let down."

"You're drunk," Jordan accused.

"No, I'm right," Will said firmly. He looked into Jordan's eyes and could see a dangerous glint growing in them. "I just don't want to see you end up like your pops."

"I won't," Jordan growled. His hand shook slightly as he brought another shot to his lips.

"You're almost there," Will said carelessly.

"Shut up," Jordan spoke through clenched teeth. Will was persistent though.

"He started off just like you, now look at him," Will said.

"Shut up," Jordan's voice oozed with venom. He downed another shot.

"You can save yourself, Jordan. You don't have to be stuck like he is—like everyone is in this damn place. Look around, you really want to be sitting at the same bar, drunk on a Wednesday night at forty? I sure as hell don't."

Jordan didn't reply, choosing to ignore his friend. Will wasn't having it.

"If you don't do something, you'll be looking at yourself in the mirror thirty years from now and all you'll see is your father. All you'll see is him looking back at you with the same drunk, angry eyes."

Jordan's fist knocked Will down onto the floor before he could say another word. No one around seemed to notice the conflict, everyone in the bar was wrapped up in their own downward spiral.

Will stood to his feet and looked sadly at his friend. He put up his hands in surrender. He was done fighting. "They all start out just like us," his voice was soft, "and they all get stuck." He wiped the blood from his lips. "Neither of us deserves to be stuck." With that, Will left and Jordan took one last shot.

The air was brisk and brutal, but the warmth the alcohol provided flowed through Jordan's body, shielding him from the cold of the night. The one thing the drinks didn't do for Jordan though was keep him oblivious to how black the sky seemed. Tonight, for some reason, the sky not only looked black but felt so much darker and more hopeless than usual.

Every breath Jordan released was shaky and uncertain. He stumbled along the dimly lit streets and he thought of his mom falling apart at the seams. He thought of Will—the only friend he had ever had. He even thought of Ali, the poor girl, looking for affection from a guy who didn't even care to know her last name.

And he thought of his father. Always leaving them and then barging back in and making everything worse. When he was gone Sarah would get so much better, she would sober up, start working more, then Gabriel would waltz back in when he ran out of money and bring his drugs right back under Sarah's nose. He was a terrible person and a terrible father.

"Daddy," Jordan had said when he was just a little kid holding onto the straps of his backpack, "wanna know what I wanna be when I grow up?" Gabriel didn't answer, the TV was more important than his son, but Jordan continued to tell him, "A doctor! I wanna be a doctor."

This caught Gabriel's attention. He turned his head toward Jordan with a chuckle. "You can't," he told the ten-year-old. Jordan's excitement shattered.

"Why?" his voice cracked as he asked.

"You're not smart enough and we don't have the money to send you to college for that. Not to mention, no one wants a troublemaking kid walking around with a lab coat and a scalpel."

"I'm not a troublemaking kid," Jordan said in defense.

"Yeah, you are, and you'll only get worse." Gabriel turned back to the TV with a beer in his hand.

Jordan kicked over a metal trash can at the memory. His father had left when Jordan started high school and Sarah had actually encouraged him about being a doctor. Science classes and the medical field had always interested him. He used to work hard at those classes, used to impress his teachers with his grades. Then reality settled in when his father came home, halfway through his high school years. He was reminded of his father's words every day and the dream died.

And now, he found himself in the alleyway with his left elbow propped up on his knee as he brought his right hand up to his mouth to take a hit. He was debating about going to find Will and apologize.

From the corner of his eye, four figures were making their way toward him. He didn't recognize any of the guys, but he knew from the looks on their faces that they wanted to draw blood and Jordan was their target.

"I don't have anything on me," he told them. They continued moving in. Jordan tried to look intimidating—he was usually quite good at it—but with the world slightly spinning, he was just looking like an idiot. He started to back up, only to trip over himself.

In a blink of an eye, Jordan was pinned to the ground enduring kicks and punches. One pair of hands was digging into his pockets taking out his barren wallet, knife, and even his empty package of gum. Jordan's fist shot up and hit one of the guys in the mouth. He then kicked another guy and somehow managed to stand up and take a few steps away from the group.

Suddenly he was pushed against a wall and felt something sharp and cool against his throat. It was his own knife being lightly pressed against his skin. He used his elbow to knock the knife out of the guy's hand and it fell to the ground. Jordan kicked his opponent's legs out from under him and straddled him. He threw punches into the face below him.

Jordan was then picked up and thrown to the ground with a resounding crack when his head hit the concrete. He got up and tried to steady himself. Everything was blurry as he lunged at the guy who had thrown him down.

At the same time that sirens began to wail somewhere nearby, a sharp pain made Jordan scream out. His attackers took off running as Jordan slumped to the ground. He put his hand to where the pain was and felt a hot sticky substance. He grasped the handle of his knife and pulled it out.

He screamed out in agonizing pain.

He began to feel light-headed. All he could think about for some reason was officer Blight. Though Jordan gave the officer a constant attitude, he was the only man Jordan had any respect for. The only man that Jordan would ever want to be like; Blight was still an idiot though. He was an idiot to think that Jordan was capable of achieving something in his life. He was an idiot for believing in Jordan—for believing in a dumb kid.

The world started blacking out. Jordan tried to keep his eyes open, but they weighed a ton. He knew he was losing a lot of blood, he knew his head was in bad shape, and he knew that the dumpster across from him could very well be the last thing he would ever see.

Maybe he was okay with that. Maybe it would be better for him to just die. It would mean one less screwed up kid in the world. It would mean one less troublemaker for the law to deal with. It would mean one less dead-end dreamer.

Jordan drew in a sharp breath.

His body shook.

His head ached.

His blood soaked his clothes.

His blood soaked the ground.

His thoughts stopped short.

CHAPTER 6. RECRUITMENT

The man with the top hat lifted Jordan up and brought him a couple of steps away from the group after Jordan sent a kick to one of his attackers. Jordan was then able to fight back a little more, though he was still unsteady on his feet. Everything was happening so fast, Jordan was pushed against the wall and thrown down so hard the sidewalk could've cracked from the impact.

"NO!" the man yelled. Jordan screamed out in unbelievable pain and the wail of sirens startled the attackers. The guys ran off to leave Jordan to bleed to death.

The man sat in the alleyway beside Jordan holding his hand, though he knew Jordan had no clue he was there. Jordan blinked a couple of times, his chest heaved, his breaths were short. His gray t-shirt was now mostly dark red.

"I'm so sorry, Jordan," the man said through his own tears. "You deserve better than this. You will have better than this." The dark bland alley was colored for a moment with red smoke.

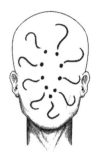

CHAPTER 7. MICHAEL

"I'm not gonna spend this weekend at home, man." Michael's closest friend James spoke through the phone. "My mom and her boyfriend have been screaming at each other all week, I need a break."

"I heard Scott's throwing a party but I'll be pissed if I end up being designated driver again." Michael continued to doodle on his rough draft of a college essay.

His mother had him practicing them over and over all summer long. "Michael, these essays determine your future! This is no joke!" she had yelled numerous times after he handed her another incomplete paper.

"Well then, let's just stay at his place. His mom is somewhere in Europe anyway."

"Yeah, I guess."

"Michael!" He heard his mother call from downstairs.

"I gotta go, I'll pick you up around nine."

They ended their call and Michael took his sweet time going downstairs where his mother was sitting in her favorite chair with a glass of expensive white wine and a designer clothing magazine in hand.

"Yeah?" he asked her.

She didn't look up from her magazine, "Your brother will be here for dinner tonight."

Michael groaned.

"Michael," Elizabeth reprimanded. She looked at her son disapprovingly.

"I have plans tonight. I'm picking James up later."

"Well, we're eating at seven so that should give you plenty of time to socialize with your family and then go waste another night doing meaningless things with meaningless people."

Michael was about to retort, but his mother's attention was caught by their house cleaner, Beth. She told her, "Don't forget to dust the china, I need it for a dinner party on Sunday." Beth replied with a 'yes ma'am' and walked over to the china cabinet.

Michael rolled his eyes at his pretentious mother. Her focus went back to her magazine, "You know, Robby is very good at dividing up his time wisely, you should ask him for tips. Time management is a very important skill that will take you far in life."

"Yes, I would love to hear how he manages to be such an amazing son and such an infuriating douchebag all at once."

"Michael!"

"Mother!" he mocked as he returned to his bedroom.

With his parents, it was always Robby this and Robby that. He had always wondered why they even bothered having another kid when they already had the "perfect" son. Michael sat down at his desk and looked at his college essay. There was one poorly written paragraph about absolutely nothing at all. He didn't even remember writing it in the first place.

His parents were making him apply to so many different colleges he couldn't even keep track. "It's best to have options," his father told him, except none of them were options chosen by Michael. The prompt for the essay in front of him was asking what he would do with the education he would receive.

"I don't know yet," he answered aloud. It seemed everybody wanted answers right here and now, but Michael didn't have any. He didn't know what his next step was, he knew he would take one eventually, he just had no idea where. The thought of the future made him want to curl up under the covers and not move at all.

He remembers the feeling of constant pressure while growing up. The pressure to make his parents look good, to make the team, get good grades, look nice, speak properly—to live the life his family had determined for him. It felt like his life was a never-ending cycle of work and stress and failing to meet everyone's expectations. A small voice inside whispered, *There has to be more than this.*

He closed the apps on his phone and realized it was 6:50 and that his mother was going to call him to dinner at any moment.

He took the time to store up any and all sarcastic comments. He heard the door open downstairs, low voices and hands patting backs followed right after. Robby was home. Michael could hear his mother cooing over her son that she saw less than three weeks ago. His Ivy league school was only a half-hour from home so he came back way too often.

"Michael, dinner!" He walked into the dining room where everyone was already seated. His father and Robby sat at each end of the table, and Michael sat across from his mother, preparing to endure an hour or so of pure hell.

He greeted no one and no one greeted him. Robby continued to talk as if Michael hadn't just walked in. His mother and father ate up every word and looked at Robby with pride. Michael wanted to gouge his eyes out and cut off his ears.

"So, Michael, what's your number one?" Robby finally broke the ice and acknowledged his younger brother's presence.

"Desire?"

Robby was not amused. "What's your number one college?"

"Oh." He took a drink of his soda. "I don't know." He let out a low burp purposely just to get the signature glare from his mother. His father ignored him.

"Well, you should decide soon, you're about to be in the application season," Robby said.

"Well, my pen is locked and loaded." Michael pointed his fork at Robby and imitated the sound of a gun being loaded and fired.

"It's too bad they don't give scholarships for being a smart ass," Robby said with harshness in his voice that his parents would never reprimand. They never had.

"I'm sure they do. Didn't you get one for being a kiss a—"

"Boys," Christopher's authoritative voice boomed cutting Michael off. "Enough." He only faced Michael, his jaw ticking letting it be known that he was fed up.

"Robby, whatever happened to that sweet young lady you were seeing?" Elizabeth asked as she swished her third glass of wine around.

"Did she realize she basically would've married Biff from *Back to the Future*?" Michael said quickly.

"Michael, you will not speak another word at this table." Michael stared into the cold eyes of his father, refusing to be the first to look away. Elizabeth drew her husband's attention towards her when she asked Robby about the college's political opportunities and whether or not he'd be running for office.

Of all the families I could've been born into, Michael thought to himself. *I don't belong here, I never have.*

For the rest of the dinner, Michael played back parts of his favorite movies in his head and moved his food around his plate with his fork. This was nothing new, every family dinner that he could ever remember happened something like this. No one even bothered to glance at Michael for the rest of the meal. He convinced himself he didn't care. He didn't even like his family, so why should it matter whether or not they liked him? But he couldn't shake the twisting feeling in his stomach and the tightening in his throat.

"Michael, will you help me with the dishes before you go?" Elizabeth asked.

Michael got up and started clearing the table with his mother. His father and brother went and sat in the living room, probably to discuss how immature and irresponsible Michael was. He stood next to his mom at the sink.

"I wish you would learn to control your tongue. Robby did not deserve those comments." she shook her head as she spoke.

Michael stayed silent.

"He was just being interested in your life. It wouldn't hurt if you would show some interest in his."

Michael handed her a plate.

"I am not a fan of monologues, *Michael.*"

"I'm just controlling my tongue, *mother.*"

Elizabeth sighed and looked out of the kitchen window dramatically. She waved her hand dismissing him. "Just go."

Michael walked passed the living room twirling his key chain around his pointer finger.

"Where are you going?" Christopher demanded. Michael slipped his jacket on.

"Out." Michael kept his back to his father but he could feel his angry glare.

"You're not going to apologize for making a scene at dinner?"

Michael opened the front door as he spoke, "Are you going to apologize for making an ass of a son?"

"Are you referring to yourself or your successful, dean's list, older brother?" Christopher stood and walked toward the door, grabbed Michael's shoulder and turned him to face him. "You watch how you speak to me boy,"—he squeezed his shoulder tightly, threateningly—"understood?"

"Understood," Michael said through clenched teeth. He slammed the door behind him.

Michael seethed the entire drive to James' house. He didn't put on any music, he sped past every car, and almost ran a couple of lights. His father knew just how to get under his skin. He matched Michael's sarcasm but had an extra dose of venom in every word. He was plain old mean. He rolled his shoulder that Christopher had grabbed. He had never really laid a hand on him, just hard grips, mean glares, and the occasional smack to the back of the head. He wouldn't be surprised if he ever did though.

His mother always tried to defend his father, saying that he had a rough childhood because his father had been very hard on him. Michael couldn't understand the logic of becoming a mean father because you were raised by one. Having a father like Christopher made Michael want to be the complete opposite. It shouldn't have excused Christopher at all.

"You're early," James said when he opened his front door.

"I had to get out of there." His friend gave a questioning look. "Robby's home."

"Oh." James put his jacket on.

"Let's get food before we go, I'm starving," Michael said. James nodded in agreement.

The party was mediocre. It was the same routine they had been living all throughout high school. Drink some, smoke some, make out some, fight some, and then do it all over again. It was the same jerks, and the same girls, and the same drama. Michael mostly kept to himself that night, still angry from the dinner. He poured drink after drink, not even paying attention to how much alcohol and how little of anything else was in the cups.

Michael checked the time on his phone but the numbers blurred together. He looked around for James and saw he was preoccupied with a girl. By the time Michael made it to the front yard, his cup had been knocked into so many times there was nothing left in it. He stumbled around the yard, breathing in the fresh air, trying to make the world stop spinning. He replayed the scene at dinner in his mind. He cursed Robby for casting such a big shadow over him, cursed his parents for making it insufferable to be a part of that family, and cursed the universe for putting him there.

Deep down, though he would never admit it, he was jealous of Robby. Jealous at how easy it all came to him. Jealous of the purpose that he had always seemed to have felt. Robby knew what he wanted and went after it. Yeah, he was a jerk, but he was a jerk with ambition. Michael wished that he could feel ambitious about something, anything.

Being so immersed in thought, Michael lost his footing, tripped, and landed right next to a passed out classmate. He rolled onto his back and looked up at the stars. There were so many of them. He once read that most of the stars seen at night were actually dead, and had been for millions of years, but they still shined. Suddenly, he was overwhelmed and unable to look into the stars that forever made their mark on the galaxy.

Michael had no concept of time as he lay frighteningly still on the grass with his eyes closed.

"Dude, are you alive?" James lightly touched Michael's shoulder with his foot.

"Literally or figuratively?" Michael kept his eyes closed as he spoke.

"Umm," James wrinkled his face as he tried to remember what either of those words meant.

"Literally yes, figuratively no. It's like, I'm standing completely still while the world spins wildly around me. Everyone is fast-paced and I'm in slow motion. What am I even doing here? What purpose do I serve? Is there more than this? What kind of mark am I going to leave on this planet? I'm just a shadow while everyone else is a neon ray of light. So, I guess I'm not alive. I'm breathing and talking and walking, but I am nothing."

"Bro, what is coming out of your mouth right now?" James rubbed his head; all this deep thinking was going to give him a worse hangover than the liquor. The boys could hear someone throwing up not too far from them. "I just came to tell you that I'm going home with Dana."

"Dana, who?" Michael stood up and held onto James to balance himself.

"Dana, you know, Dana."

"Oh, yeah." Michael had no idea who James was talking about. "Have fun."

James smirked and nodded.

Michael decided to take a walk and sober up. It was too dark to be walking around on the back roads, but that was the last thing on his mind. All he could think about was his father. Robby was already a clone of Christopher, but Michael didn't want to be. He didn't want to sit in leather desk chairs and smoke cigars while maids cleaned the house. Michael had no idea who he was, but he knew exactly who he didn't want to be.

"Ow." Michael covered his eyes from bright lights not realizing where they were coming from. He felt the impact long before he put two and two together.

His body hit the pavement and his head bounced up and down as the car rolled over him. He could see someone get out of the car and he heard them scream. But then there was only darkness.

CHAPTER 8. RECRUITMENT

The man with the top hat screamed, "Michael, watch out!"

Michael didn't hear a word, didn't see a thing. Within seconds the car hit him. His mangled body lay on the road.

The car stopped and a woman got out screaming. She ran to Michael and put her ear to his mouth to check if he was breathing. He was unrecognizable. Blood covered his face, his arms were twisted in the wrong direction, the crack in his head was spilling an ocean of blood. She screamed and paced back and forth between him and her car as she called for help.

The man with the top hat ran to the broken boy and held his face in his hands. Michael was mumbling incoherently, barely alive his mind was going haywire. The woman spoke frantically on the phone. As soon as her back was turned, R.L. hugged Michael close to him and they disappeared leaving no trace behind.

CHAPTER 9. ZOE

Her beat-up sneakers rested against the windshield as her mother pulled into their driveway. She wore the same shoes every day and it was showing. The once white color was now brown, the dirt staining the sides. The laces were frayed and needed to be replaced.

"Zoe, we're going to have to talk about this."

Zoe huffed and continued to stare at her feet.

"Don't be like that with me! This is a big deal! You've been in two fights this month. What is going on with you?"

Zoe looked out of the car window and held her tongue. Her mind flashed back to the fistfight that had erupted in the parking lot of her school that afternoon. One minute she was standing by herself and the next she was on top of some girl delivering punch after punch into her face.

Zoe couldn't stop, even though she knew she should've. She liked the power she felt, having the upper hand for once. Zoe relished in those moments where she was not on the receiving end. She gently touched her bruised knuckles remembering how scared the other girl looked. Guilt made her stomach uneasy and she closed her eyes.

Zoe wanted so badly to tell her mother everything, to show her the bruises on her stomach and legs, but she couldn't. She had to be strong. Her mom was dealing with enough of her own problems. She took a deep breath, held her tears at bay, and opened her eyes, focusing on their overgrown front yard.

"Zoe," her mother demanded answers.

"Nothing," she kept her voice steady, "Nothing is wrong."

Jennifer sighed. Like so many times before, she gave up on trying to communicate with her daughter. *When she's ready she'll open up,* she thought to herself. "I have to get back to the office. I'll be home late but there are leftovers in the fridge." She patted her daughter's knee and wondered why she had flinched but didn't ask.

Zoe reluctantly got out of the car and went into her quaint, blue shutter, white picket fence, lie of a house. She tried to be as quiet as humanly possible while making her way up the stairs. She figured her stepfather, Paul, was held up in his room working. He was a freelance journalist, which seemed cool when she first met him. Now she resented the job since it kept him home most of the time.

She sat on her bed with her notebook to her right and her laptop to her left. She went back and forth between the two, perusing through social media and jotting down her poetic thoughts when inspiration hit.

Cracks on my innocent skin,
Again and again and again.
Rips in my fragile soul,
Please no, no.
Bruises on my lonely heart,
I am torn apart.
Completely apart.

Zoe sighed. Lately, everything she had been writing had sounded so broken. She despised it. Taking a deep breath, she tried to focus on positive things. She tried to force herself into the happiness she wanted so badly.

Blue sky
Bright lights
Birds fly –
Home.
Wise moon
White room
Where are you –
Alone.

"Ugh!" She closed her notebook in frustration and shoved it off her bed. The sudden turning of her brass doorknob sparked a wildfire of fear inside her. She stayed silent, staring at her computer screen, praying that Paul would leave her alone.

"Zoe, how was your day?" To her dismay, he continued taking slow steps forward. She wanted to puke at the sound of his voice, "I'm talking to you kid," He said harshly.

She continued to ignore him, knowing it would do no good. She yelped when his hands grabbed her shoulders and pressed her into the bed. Panic flashed through her.

"Get off!" She yelled. She kicked and squirmed and screamed. His fist connecting with her body kept her beneath him as he had his way.

"Shut up!" He shouted in her ear. Zoe closed her eyes so tight it hurt.

He always steered clear of her face, not wanting people to ask questions. He had been getting away with this for six months. Zoe had to learn how to escape her reality through her mind. She would think about the future. Just one more year and she'd be as far away as middle-class money could take her. She would be on a beautiful campus with friends, real genuine friends, and she would laugh and enjoy the sunshine on her clean unbruised body. She would finally be happy because she would be gone.

Paul closed her bedroom door behind him. Zoe laid still for a few moments before opening her eyes and letting the tears escape. She hated crying. She just wanted to be okay. She just wanted to be able to get over it. She didn't want to be that girl who sobbed behind closed doors, the girl who felt alone and worthless. Nonetheless, that's who she had become.

After standing beneath a scalding hot shower and scrubbing her body till it was raw, Zoe picked up her notebook. She had so many emotions swirling inside, she had to get them out somehow. She didn't want to cry, and she sure didn't want to tell anyone. So, she let her pen move along the lined pages frantically.

Nothing's fair, Why me?
That world out there, What's it like to be free?
This girl here, Who am I to deserve this?
Nothing's fair, Where is my innocence?

Her stomach growled but Zoe didn't dare get out of bed. Her last thoughts before drifting into sleep were of her real father. His soft features, soothing voice, and a warm smile. His contagious laugh, strong hugs, and a sense of fun. His brown hair, hazel eyes and the excruciatingly easy way he walked right out of her life and never looked back.

The next morning she pulled on her jeans and sweatshirt, the same thing she wore every day. She had stopped wearing shorts and skirts when Paul moved in. She hated the attention they drew, so she did her best to make herself look unappealing. It never worked though.

She walked down the stairs into the kitchen and wanted to scream at her mother. She sat there with Paul at the table. Coffee cups in hand, giggling and looking into each other's eyes. It was revolting. Zoe grabbed a pop tart and a water bottle, said a quick goodbye to her mom, and got out of the house.

She kept her head down and headphones in as she navigated through the school hallways to her locker. When she opened it, empty water bottles stood side by side like an army in front of a pile of ripped folders and blank notebooks. She just stared into the chaos that she imagined to be the physical representation of her life. She was torn and blank and empty. She was stuck inside a metal box with a lock to keep everyone out and all her baggage in.

"Ow." Zoe rubbed the spot on her shoulder that had been pushed against her locker door. Her whole body was in pain from the night before. "Watch where you're going!" She snapped.

The group turned around to look at her. They flipped her off and laughed as they walked away.

She cursed at them loudly, wanting them to come back. She needed to get her anger out. They didn't bother to look at her.

The bell rang and she joined the students of her high school in the motions of the day. It wasn't until the fifth period that the guidance counselor called her to her office to address the slight altercation from the day before.

"So what was your logical reasoning this time?" Mrs. Valencia beckoned Zoe to the plush olive green armchair.

"She called me a slut." Zoe sat cross-legged.

"So you just go and punch her? Because of one word?"

"That word hurt, right here." Sarcastically, Zoe put her hand to her heart.

"Cut the crap." Mrs. Valencia pulled up a chair and sat knee to knee with Zoe. "What's really going on?"

"Nothing is going on." Zoe laughed and rolled her eyes.

Mrs. Valencia wasn't fooled. "Is something happening at home?"

Zoe was suddenly at a loss for words. She couldn't help but drop her mouth out of shock. She mentally debated being truthful. She had always liked Mrs. Valencia and talked to her about little things, but how did this high school guidance counselor expect Zoe to reveal what's been eating her alive? How was Zoe supposed to divulge her pain when she could barely come to terms with it herself? The answer was simple, she couldn't.

"What do you mean?" Just as quickly as Zoe was caught off guard, she had put her calm and collected armor on.

"Is it your stepfather? Are he and your mom fighting? Is he hurting her? Is he hurting you?" Mrs. Valencia fired question after question, noticing the flickers of fear and disgust that appeared in Zoe's eyes.

Mrs. Valencia had been with Zoe long enough to know that something was wrong. She showed no signs of physical abuse but there were signs of something troubling her. The violence, the attitude, the lack of friends or involvement in anything extracurricular. She knew Zoe was hiding her true self, hiding what was going on. Mrs. Valencia was determined not to let this girl waste away and miss her opportunity to be something great.

"No," Zoe's voice was barely above a whisper.

"Please, Zoe, I can help you. I want to help you, but you have to talk to me." *Please.* Mrs. Valencia echoed in her mind. She wanted so badly to help, but Zoe had to open the door.

Zoe closed her eyes. Inhale, exhale. "I'm okay." Her mouth was dry and her throat was closing up. She gave her best shot at convincing Mrs. Valencia, and herself. "Everything's okay." She even managed a smile.

"You're lying."

"I am not!" Now Zoe was getting annoyed. Why wouldn't this lady just give up?

"Look, I know you're scared, but you need to trust me. If he's hurting you or your mom we can help you, I can make it stop. He belongs in jail."

The scene played out in Zoe's head: flashing lights outside her suburban home, cuffs tight around Paul's wrists, officers interrogating Zoe, and her mother distraught and depressed at the loss of another husband. And it would be Zoe's fault, all over again.

She stood at the sound of the bell. "I'm fine." Ignoring the pleas for truth, Zoe barreled down the school hallway to sixth-period algebra.

Broken but unspoken, no one can ever know.

Shameful and painful, hands held tight, how do I let go?

The words were scribbled in the margins of her math notebook. Writing always helped cool her down and get her mind in order. Since she was incapable of expressing herself out loud, paper was her best friend – her confidant. Her journals knew all her secrets, all her fears. Not a thing on earth knew her better.

She felt the pain in her shoulder again as a finger poked her. She hissed and looked to her left. "What?" she asked harshly.

"Damn, what crawled up your butt this morning?" Daniel smiled. He would consider the two of them to be friends but to Zoe they were acquaintances. He was always sweet to her; sweet and clueless.

"What do you want?" she softened her voice. She didn't want to be mean to him, it just happened naturally. She had become wary of the male species, she had never had a good experience with any of them.

"I was wondering if you wanted to study together for the test next week."

Zoe thought about it for a minute. She usually kept to herself, mostly because people kept away. Everyone in school knew how angry and violent she was. They didn't bother her and she didn't bother them. Everyone except for poor innocent Daniel.

"No thanks, I'm good." She turned away from the disappointed expression on his face.

She second-guessed herself for a moment, it wouldn't hurt to just spend a couple of hours with him. He had always been nice to her, how bad could it be? She began to turn back to him when her pain reminded her of her reality. She couldn't bring anyone else into it. And she definitely couldn't have a reason to stay, or ever come back to this town. Daniel wouldn't want to deal with the baggage she was carrying anyway. She kept silent as sadness settled in.

Relief hit like a tidal wave when Zoe saw her empty driveway. Paul must be out on a job, or out drinking. Or maybe he decided to bail. She was heartbroken when her father left, but when it came to Paul there was nothing she wanted more than for him to disappear forever.

It had been months since Zoe had been alone in the house. Months since she had felt safe in the home where she had grown up. She decided to take full advantage of it. After locking the front door and closing all the curtains, she plugged her phone into the surround sound stereo system and blasted all her favorite songs.

The sound of guitars and drums shook the plain walls that stood tall around her. Zoe closed her eyes and blocked everything out. She pushed the memories of Paul's forceful hands out of her mind. The synth and drum pad sounds helped her ignore the soreness of her body. She focused on rapping the verses perfectly. She got lost in the rhythm, putting her unfair situation out of her head. She let the lyrics consume her, making her feel less alone. The voices of the singers making her feel like maybe she wasn't the only broken one.

But then again, maybe she was.

She shook her head and told herself to stop thinking so much. She sang at the top of her lungs. She danced around, using a water bottle as a microphone. She played along with the instruments in the air. She imagined she was on a stage at a sold-out show. She lost all sense of time—all sense of reality—she was in her own impenetrable bubble.

She was safe. She was having fun. She was momentarily content.

Until the music stopped.

Zoe's entire body froze at the sound of applause. She turned around to a smiling, drunk Paul. His eyes were sinister. The sun had begun to set, causing Shadows to occupy the walls and the face of the man that made Zoe wish she had never been born.

"Fantastic show. How about an encore?" He started walking towards her and she choked at the smell of liquor on him. She took quick steps backward and he grabbed her arm. "Where do you think you're going?"

"Stop," she whispered.

"What was that?" He yanked her forward.

"Stop," Zoe's voice was louder this time.

He chuckled and tightened his grip. His other arm slid around her waist. She jerked back and used all her strength to push him away. She took off up the stairs. Paul stood still for a moment, blinking in disbelief. He gripped the railing to keep his balance as he followed her. He was going to make her pay for that.

Drops of water leaked from the bathtub faucet. Zoe sat in the tub with her head resting between her knees. She let out a tiny scream when Paul started knocking on the bathroom door. She hugged her knees tightly. The door shook from the contact with his fists. Zoe's breath was quickening. This was the only place she could think to hide. She covered her ears to ignore his knocking.

She began to mutter, "It won't last forever, darling it will get better."

"Zoe!" She flinched at Paul's scream. "Zoe, open this damn door!" Her mumbling got louder. "NOW!" he yelled.

"The sun might not be shining right now, but don't worry, it's only hidden behind a few clouds." These words brought her slivers of comfort. Words she had written and rewritten dozens of times, words she made herself believe even when it seemed useless.

"Zoe, you better open this door now or else! Zoe! ZOE!" Paul's voice was manic. He was hitting the door so hard it was bound to break any moment. Her voice was raised enough for him to hear.

"It won't be too long now, you'll get out, you'll get out, I promise you'll get out!" her voice was strained and cracked.

Paul's hands were sore as he hit the door over and over. He screamed her name. She screamed her words. "It won't last forever, darling it will get better." She needed to hear her own voice above his.

"It'll be okay! It'll be okay! You'll be okay!" Tears streamed down her face. Her head was in excruciating pain from the overwhelming noise. "It'll be okay! It'll be okay!" She was lost in her mind, no longer in the real world. "It'll be okay! You'll be okay!"

Zoe noticed that her voice was now the only one echoing throughout the house. "Hidden behind a few clouds," she whispered.

She felt as though she were in a haze. It seemed like an hour before Zoe mustered up enough strength to stand. Her shaking hand turned the doorknob and she stepped into an empty hallway.

An eerie quiet met her ears. She saw that her mom's bedroom door was closed. She should be home from work any minute. Paul wouldn't be stupid enough to do anything at this time of night.

Every step she took farther away from that door, farther away from Paul, the more capable of breathing she became. Stepping into her bedroom she immediately knew something was wrong. She scanned her surroundings. By the time she saw him standing right next to her, it was too late. He shoved her into her dresser. She cried out in pain and fell to the floor. She tried to crawl away, but Paul grabbed her legs. He hit her, and hit her, and hit her. For the first time, he didn't care about her face.

"Thought you could get away?" There was no stopping him. He was in an uncontrollable rage.

With one last burst of energy and courage, Zoe sent a kick to Paul's stomach and took off past him to the stairs. He was right on her heels. As she was about to take the first step down, he grabbed her shoulders and pressed her against the wall.

"Stupid girl," he whispered.

She turned to get away from the force of his hands. They fought back and forth. The next thing she knew, there was a loud crack and she was lying on the first floor. Her body was in a painfully awkward position. She felt blood soaking her hair and dripping down her forehead. She looked up to see a blurry Paul standing at the top of the stairs, his eyes wide with realization.

At that moment, Zoe had never wanted her dad more. *If only I had done more to make him stay.* She remembered the fights between her parents, the screaming, the breaking of things. She remembers her mother's accusations that her father had been cheating.

"I'm not happy here!" he had screamed.

Zoe sat in her bedroom doorway crying. Why didn't she make her father happy? She had tried. She did well in school and she followed the rules, but he wasn't happy.

"Leave then! Leave us! We don't need you!" her mom screamed back.

Zoe hated her mother for saying those words. I need him, she wanted to say. But she didn't. She didn't speak up. She didn't beg him not to leave.

She thought as she laid on the floor, *maybe I deserve this. Maybe this is the Universe's way of telling me I'm no good, of telling me I'm worthless.*

The world was blacking in and out. She heard her mother scream. Paul was still at the top of the stairs, he hadn't moved a muscle. Jennifer's hands cupped her daughter's face as she cried. Out of her glossed lips came comforting words. Words assuring the broken girl that it would be okay.

It was too late for it to be okay though.

CHAPTER 10. RECRUITMENT

The man with the top hat stood in the living room and watched as Jennifer held Zoe's face in her hands. Paul was still at the top of the stairs muttering incoherently.

"What have you done?!" Jennifer's screaming voice cracked with emotion. "What have you done?!" she kept saying.

She fumbled for her cell phone and dialed 911. She told them to hurry, told them that her daughter fell down the stairs, told them that she had stopped breathing.

Paul took a step down and Jennifer screamed at him to stay where he was, "Don't you dare come any closer!" her voice was frantic. Whispering Zoe's name, shaking her gently, kissing her forehead. Blood covered her hands as she cradled her daughter's head.

Sirens and lights awakened the dark street, no doubt causing everyone on the block to peek out from behind their curtains. Jennifer jumped up and ran out of the house to flag the paramedics down.

The man walked quickly to Zoe. Paul was sitting at the top of the stairs, visibly shaking. Zoe's body was limp in the man's arms as he picked her up. He left behind only a cloud of glittery red smoke.

CHAPTER 11. LADIES AND GENTLEMEN

"Ladies and gentlemen." The Ringleader's voice filled the Big Top, but he could not be seen. "Boys and girls." Colorful lights darted across the excited audience. "Children of all ages." The children bounced up and down with cotton candy in hand. "Tonight we will steal you away from your world. We will invade your mind, your heart, and your dreams. Miracles will materialize right before your very eyes," the Ringleader's voice evoked curiosity.

"Here at this circus, we believe that the impossible is possible!" his voice got louder, "there is no such thing as ordinary, no such thing as average! Tonight you will experience freedom! Freedom from human logic. Freedom from what you think you know. You are entering a place from which you will never wish to leave!"

The faint music that had been playing behind him, got louder and more intense. Massive colorful posters of various circus acts hung from the top of the tent, slightly swaying back and forth. Bleachers holding thousands of people were arranged in a circle with the band settled in an orchestra pit.

"It is my pleasure and my privilege." The lights went red and expanded across the audience in the stands. "To welcome you all." The crowd went wild. "To Cirque." The drums echoed. "Des." Smoke began to rise from the ground of the circus ring. "Élus," the Ringleader bellowed as the band played. Lights flashed every color imaginable and the audience stood to their feet cheering.

A navy blue curtain, covered with sparkling silver stars, opened for the Ringleader to enter through it. He was riding a larger than life gold unicycle. He wore a purple pea coat, a black top hat, and a huge smile. The lights reflected off of the stripes of silver on his coat. He rode around waving to the audience and encouraging the musicians to play louder.

"Greetings! I am the Ringleader here at Cirque Des Élus!" Sparkling fireworks went off all around the audience. The response was happy screams and clapping. "We have quite a show for you tonight. So sit tight and open your mind," he spoke animatedly, gesturing with his hands and widening his eyes. "To kick off our adventure, take a deep breath, and feast your eyes to the sky!" He raised his right hand and his head straight up and all the lights went black except for the ceiling of the Big Top Tent which was illuminated with white light.

On the right side of the tent, six people stood tall on platforms wearing full-body navy blue leotards. The women had their hair pulled up, and the silver sequins that adorned their costume glimmered in the spotlight. The men had silver stripes running up the sides of their costumes.

"Today you will see these brave, talented performers swing from bar-to-bar, person-to-person, limb-to-limb, at an unbelievable fifty feet in the air! Here they are, the highly regarded, Masters of the Trapeze!" the Ringleader's voice spoke from the darkness and all attention was focused solely upward.

Two bars hung from the ceiling, one on the left, one on the right. A seventh Trapeze Artist was lowered right in between them, hanging upside down with the backs of his knees resting on the bar. He began swinging back and forth. Another performer stood at the edge of the lowest of the two platforms on the left side, awaiting the perfect moment to leap forward. The audience gasped as she threw herself into the air and grabbed ahold of his hands. They swung back and forth. Every so often she would let go of him and flip to grab onto another bar that had been lowered. There was a pit in every audience member's stomach as they watched.

More trapeze bars were lowered from the ceiling and the Trapeze Artists jumped into the act. They went back and forth swinging off of one another, doing flips and adding more people to their count until all eight people were soaring above the audience.

All of the Trapeze Artists continued earning gasps and crazed applause as they leaped, and swung, and flipped, and grabbed onto each other. The drums began beating faster, signaling the finale. The spotlight turned to a woman who stood on a platform ten feet higher than her fellow trapeze family. She lifted her arms in the air and dived from the platform. The bar that was waiting for her, was lowered incredibly close to the ground. She flipped and spun at least ten times before grasping onto the bar and swinging with her legs out in front of her, barely missing the ground.

She continued to swing and flip as the bar was raised to the platform where the other artists waited. She flipped once more and as soon as she landed, the crowd gave a standing ovation clapping and cheering wildly.

The spotlight above shut off as deep intense drumming again flowed from the band. A dozen men and women dressed in all black marched to the middle of the ring and stood shoulder to shoulder in a circle. A dark red light covered them. In the middle of the group was a giant black fire pit that they had rolled out with them. The Fire Breathers all bowed their heads and as soon as they did a fire erupted in the middle of the pit.

Their boots shook the ground as they stomped along with the drums. There were faint specks of orange and red in their black clothing that could only be seen when the light moved across them a certain way. Their hair was gelled back and a curved design was painted on both sides of their faces, from their foreheads to their chins.

A light shone on the Ringleader as he stood on an elevated platform in the middle of the orchestra pit. His voice was deep and serious, "And now, arguably the most dangerous force of nature will be thrown, touched, swallowed, and controlled. With no protection between them and the flame, I present, the Fire Breathers." The light went off of him and the Fire Breathers again became the focus of attention.

In their left hands was a black torch. They all turned and walked in sync to the pit and lit the torches. They then turned back around and walked a few feet away from the pit and tossed the torch to their right hand. Then they increased the pace. Left, then right, then left, then right, then back and forth between performers. They arranged themselves face-to-face in two single-file lines. Some tossed the torches high, some tossed them low. To the audience, it was a commotion of orange and red.

Gasps left every mouth as the group disassembled and tossed the torches far behind their backs toward the crowd. Just when each section of the audience thought they would be set ablaze, a blur of black front-flipped and caught the torch. The onlookers applauded.

The group disbanded again and each stood near the audience, all the way around the circus ring. Every Fire Breather pulled out another torch. Holding both sticks in their left hand, they took their right-hand pointer finger and thumb and reached into the flame. They held the fire between their fingers, and carried it to the other torch and lit it. The crowd applauded, not thinking it could get any more insane. The Fire Breathers twirled their torches around and caused an uproar when they swiped the fire across their tongues.

"No way!" One parent shouted while watching with eyes and mouth wide open. The Fire Breathers put a torch into their mouth and held onto the burning end with their teeth. They took the torch out and did it again with the other one. They then went back and forth with their torches breathing on each and expanding the flame far out in front of them.

The group held both flaming torches in one hand, lifted them up and turned so their right shoulders were facing the audience, and opened their mouths. Slowly they put one torch in their mouths at a time, they disappeared down their throats and came out flameless. The Fire Breathers, with their mouths closed tightly, turned once again to face the mesmerized audience. Each performer stomped as they moved back toward the pit in the middle.

Stomp.   Stomp.   Stomp.

Each heart in the stands pounded along with the thuds echoing around them.

Stomp.   Stomp.   Stomp.

The red and white tent slightly trembled.

Stomp.   Stomp.   Stomp.

Everything went quiet. Then, standing shoulder to shoulder in a circle with their heads tilted backward the Fire Breathers lived up to their title. The lights went out. Then every mouth opened and a stream of fire escaped and illuminated the circus tent. The flames lit up the eyes of starstruck children and dumbfounded adults. There was wild applause and cheers when the fire subsided and the lights came back on. The group took their bows and left marching to the drums.

"That was unbelievable!" several people shouted.

"From the plains of India, we present the Mighty Brutus, the Lovely Evangeline, and the Precious Marco." Upbeat music and three elephants followed the Ringleader's introduction. They all wore colorful jewels and clothes, as did the people standing on top of their backs doing all sorts of tricks while keeping their balance. The child that stood on Marco did a handstand while the baby elephant held Evangeline's tail as they followed behind Brutus. After making a full circle, the majestic creatures lined up and stood on their hind legs.

They each took a turn blowing their nature-given trumpet. Brutus' was deep and assertive, followed by the strong cry of Evangeline. Precious Marco was nothing compared to his parents, but it made no difference. His tiny trunk drew "aw's" from the audience and left the children begging for an elephant as a pet.

The elephant trainers did a flip off of the elephants back and brought in yellow and white performance balls in different sizes. Each trainer whistled for their elephant and the elephants stepped forward and put one leg at a time on the ball until they were standing on it. Brutus started rolling first, Evangeline followed, and Marco rolled on after them. They went around the circus ring three times following their trainers' commands. Then all three came to a stop and gave out a loud trumpet one last time.

As the elephants left, a line of four dogs came through the curtains as different sized hoops were rolled in and placed one after another with a small platform in between them. The hoops were lit on fire and the dogs each took their turn jumping through the hoops, with the hoops all getting more narrow as they progressed. When the dogs would make it to the platforms in between the hoops they did a trick; whether it was standing on their hind legs and dancing or balancing a ball on their nose.

After the dogs jumped through all of their flaming hoops, orangutans rode in on tricycles waving to the audience and smiling wide. They did handstands on their tricycles and high-fived each other and drove off of ramps that catapulted them into the air. The audience was left in a frenzy.

CHAPTER 12. THE LIGHT

Jordan squinted as the lights moved across his face. His mind was racing trying to put the pieces together— how did he get to a circus? The man in the middle spoke to the crowd and they clapped and cheered. The circus had rolled through Jordan's city before, but he never had intentions of actually going. Was this some sort of sick joke?

"What the—" Michael's comment was cut off by the crowd roaring in anticipation to see the Trapeze Artists. He stood mesmerized by the flying people. "Insane, they're insane for doing that," he mumbled.

Drew felt nauseous as he watched the Trapeze Artists and then the Fire Breathers. It made him sick watching them do something so dangerous with smiles on their faces. *What is wrong with these people?*

Lilly clapped excitedly for everything. She "awed" and "oohed" for the animals. She had loved going to the circus with her family and seeing all the amazing crazy things.

"Excuse me," Zoe said to the people next to her. "Hello?" She tried to get the attention of the audience in front of her and behind her. They would smile and wave and then point to whatever was going on in the circus ring. *What is going on?!*

CHAPTER 13. BOYS AND GIRLS

All eyes were on the Ringleader in the center stage spotlight, "206 bones in the human body? This next act will leave you doubting that these people have any bones at all." Spotlights shone on the ground lighting up three elevated stages, the one in the middle higher than those beside it. There were two people on the high stage and one on each of the low stages standing with their hands on their hips. "See and believe, the Contortionists!"

A chime signaled the start of the Contortionists' routine. Each wore a silver bodysuit that left only the head, hands and feet bare. The performers turned to their side so their profile faced the audience. They then slowly bent backward until the back of their heads rested against their backside. The audience wowed and the Contortionists went even further to rest the top of their head on the floor and lift their legs all the way up and over until they were once again standing straight up.

Four hoops were lowered to the Contortionists and all at once they each grabbed onto one. The music played faster and faster as they each began spinning wildly while hanging from the hoops. Their legs bent this way and that way, as they slowed down and started spinning again rapidly. They lifted their legs over the top of the hoops and hung upside down, grabbing their ankles and placing them around their necks.

The hoops lowered again as the Contortionists flipped around and hung from the hoops only by their necks. They spun again and landed on the ground. The performers then gathered around each other and one girl, that was standing in the middle, suddenly went slack.

Her fellow Contortionists grabbed her arms and her legs. They threw her back and forth between the group as if she weighed nothing. Her body was limp the entire time. They twisted her arms and legs, dragged her around the circus ring, and even lifted her up above their heads and spun her around and around.

Two of the performers grabbed a very small clear case and opened it up in the middle of the ring. The girl was picked up and placed in the case by the other Contortionists. She was folded until her entire body fit perfectly inside, with the lid closed and latched. Astounded applause filled the performers' ears as the box was unlocked the girl did a backbend out of it. They stood together, smiled, took their bows, and then cartwheeled out.

"Now, lift your eyes once more! Balancing on a wire so thin they might as well be treading on air, 60 feet above the ground, the Tightrope Walkers!" The top of the circus tent was illuminated once again as two people faced each other. One on the right side of a long rope and one on the left. They wore white bodysuits with a dark purple cursive *C* on their backs and white slippers. The music began as the first step was taken.

"What happens if they fall?" a worried wife asked her husband as she gripped his arm tightly.

The rope walkers' arms were stretched horizontally to keep their balance. As the pair got closer to each other, the crowd began to whisper and murmur questions about how they would pass each other on the rope. The music paused as the walkers met each other in the middle. The walker on the right grabbed the waist of their companion, lifted them up and spun them around to the other side, allowing them to continue their cross to the platforms. The crowd cheered, some of their uneasiness diminishing.

When they were each safe on a platform the crowd erupted in cheers. Then from the left side, the Tightrope Walker held onto the handles of a wheelbarrow that had one wheel in front and one in the back, as another performer climbed in. Upbeat music started as the wheelbarrow was pushed across the tightrope with the walker that sat inside waving to the crowd below.

Next, originating from the right side, a rope walker did pirouettes all the way to the other side, followed by another one who after each step he took, dipped the opposite foot down and then brought himself up and took another step. The next performer hula hooped to the other side, followed by a woman who balanced plates on tall sticks that she held in each hand as she crossed.

As a grand finale, the performers all walked onto the rope in a line standing in a pattern of man, woman, man, woman. As soon as each couple would start walking on the ropes, the woman would grab onto the man's hands and slide slowly off the rope so that their legs dangled above the circus goers. The men continued walking along the rope while the women spun their legs, waving and smiling to the audience far below them. Once they were all on the other side they took their bows.

The applause continued long after the lights shut off and the act concluded.

"That was incredible!" the audience member's voice was drowned out by the sudden stampeding of stallions. Two-by-two, the horses ran in circles as equestrians dressed in black and white jumped from horse-to-horse. They twirled glittering lassos above them as they danced on the top of the speeding creatures.

Then, out of the curtain came three clowns on stilts making balloon animals and tossing them into the crowd. Cheerful music played loudly and colorful lights danced around the tent. Tiny cars zoomed into the arena and colorful clowns piled out juggling balls, plastic rings and even each other.

A small man with a bright blue helmet was shot out of a cannon. He landed on a trampoline where he bounced off and ended up in a clown's arms, earning a pie shoved in his face. Laughter and giddiness infected the audience.

After the circus ring cleared, the Ringleader stood near the Orchestra pit. All was dark except him. His voice lowered, "And now a simple man, with only a small switch to defend himself against sharp carnivorous teeth, will be locked inside a cage with Tyran, the king of the jungle."

Out of nowhere, as if by magic, a metal cage sat in the middle of the arena. No one had even noticed its arrival. The lion, Tyran, paced along the bars of the cage baring his teeth. A man dressed in a red jacket with gold tassels walked to the cage with a switch in hand. Against the protest of the crowd, he unlocked the door, stepped inside, and let the door lock behind him. The lion stilled and stared, his muscles tensing as this invader stood before him.

The Lion Tamer remained calm, there was nothing worrisome evident on his face. He took a bold step forward causing a rumble within Tyran. He took another step, almost a stomp, and received a warning snarl. His next step earned teeth and a pouncing stance from the animal. The man did not falter, he continued. The beast released an earth-shaking roar and the man yelled back. He continued in his advances paying no mind to the sharp drooling snout that awaited him.

When the man got close enough, Tyran lunged but was avoided with a quick sidestep to the right by the performer. They engaged in a dangerous dance of teeth and limbs. Each time Tyran braced to attack, the tamer averted with quick footing and an intense yell.

Finally, Tyran was beyond angry.

He viciously pounced forward. The man grabbed the chair that was to his right and battled the lion straight on. Tyran bit one of the legs off the chair. Loud cracks echoed as the Lion Tamer hit his switch against the metal bars of the cage. They spun around and the man jumped up on a small platform. With the chair and his switch, the tamer dominated Tyran. Standing with his foot atop the submissive beast, the audience stood to their feet and the Ringleader made his closing remarks.

"Ladies and gentlemen, we at Cirque Des Élus, thank you for joining in our adventure tonight." All of the performers and animals came out and joined him in the ring. "We hope you enjoyed yourselves and that what you have witnessed tonight leaves you truly believing this one truth—*anything* is possible and *anyone* can do the impossible. Farewell and visit us again soon!" All of Cirque took their bows. The elephants trumpeted, the horses neighed, and even Tyran let out a final resounding roar.

As the audience piled out, with much resistance from the children, a small group of teens sat on the bleachers in a cloud of confusion and wonder. The Ringleader made his way to them.

"Hello. You can call me R.L.," the Ringleader said to them.

No one said a word. R.L. smiled, despite the lack of response. He looked over each teenager, all with their mouths agape; Drew, Zoe, Jordan, Lilly, and Michael.

R.L. took a deep breath and then said, "Welcome to Cirque."

PART 2

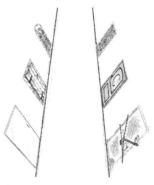

CHAPTER 14. THE TOUR

The group continued to blankly stare at the Ringleader. Up close he looked even more sensational than when he was unicycling around the circus ring. His brown hair brushed the shoulders of his dark purple pea coat. A white button-down shirt with gold buttons was tucked into gray dress pants that shimmered with tiny specks of gold.

Michael pinched himself repeatedly hoping to wake up.

"This is not a dream, Michael," R.L. spoke after noticing him.

"How do you know my name?" Michael drew out his words slowly, each laced with disbelief.

"I know all of your names." R.L. smiled softly. He was a tall, broad-shouldered man. He seemed strong yet his eyes were so soft. He was charming, with slightly crooked front teeth.

Lilly looked around, trying to put the pieces together. Zoe observed at her own arms and touched her face— she was perfectly fine. *How?* Jordan touched his stomach, no pain. He lifted up his shirt slightly and it looked like a knife had never touched his skin.

"What is this? Where are we? Who are you?!" Jordan yelled. He walked closer to R.L.

"My name is R.L. I have brought you all here to Cirque," R.L. said calmly.

Drew looked back and forth between the Ringleader and the strangers around him. *What is going on?* He thought.

"How?" Jordan tried to sound strong, tried to be assertive, but he couldn't keep his hands or lips from trembling with fear.

"I'm sure you all are confused and perhaps a bit frightened." He smiled causing slight dimples in his cheeks to appear. "But, I promise you that all will be explained. Though I can't promise everything will be understood. There is no need to be afraid, you are safe and you will come to love it here at Cirque."

"You didn't answer my question." Jordan clenched his fists.

"Believe me Jordan, you will find your answers," R.L. said softly. They stood in silence for a moment and then R.L. clapped his hands together. "Now, there is much more to see than just the Big Top. Follow me." R.L. began to walk away but no one moved. Expecting the hesitation, R.L. turned back around and raised his eyebrows in question.

"You really expect us to follow you?" Michael asked.

"Yes," R.L. replied simply with a happy expression on his face that hinted at adventure.

"No. There is no way I'm following you anywhere." Jordan walked away from the others.

"What are you doing?" Michael asked him. *This guy is trouble,* he thought after watching how Jordan acted.

"Leaving," Jordan said.

R.L. chuckled. Jordan spun around in fury. "What the hell are you laughing at!?" He yelled, "This is crazy! This isn't real!"

"This is most definitely real," R.L. told him seriously. He didn't look offended at Jordan's outburst. Jordan groaned in frustration. He fought hard against the calming effect that R.L. seemed to have.

"Where are we?" Zoe asked. Her fists were clenched tight, she could feel panic begin to rise within her chest. She had to be dreaming. She remembers her fall. She remembers her head hitting the hardwood floor with a crack. She definitely had to be dreaming right now.

R.L. looked like he was thinking for a second. He scratched his short brown beard. "You're with me." R.L. smiled and Zoe just scoffed and shook her head.

"This is crazy. This is crazy," Jordan muttered over and over as he searched for an exit.

Lilly's breathing was uneven as she rocked back and forth holding her knees to her chest. "I want to go home," Her voice was so small it was a surprise to her anyone heard it.

R.L. walked over and knelt down in front of her. "Lilly, I promise everything's going to be okay. You're—"

"How do you know our names?" Jordan yelled. "How do you know us? Who are you? And I don't want some stupid answer either!"

"Stop screaming!" Michael matched the volume of Jordan's voice and received a glare in response. Michael couldn't think with all this noise.

"Jordan," R.L. spoke softly as he stood. Jordan's hard eyes shifted targets. "I know you may be scared—"

"I am *not* scared," Jordan growled out. "*Real men don't fear.*" He shook his father's voice out of his mind. Jordan wouldn't openly admit it, but he was terrified. Fear and anger fought for dominance inside him. The more he felt afraid the more he trembled with fury.

"I know this is strange, but you *can* trust me." R.L.'s eyes were pleading, as if screaming *"Give me a chance Jordan, please, give me one chance!"*

"Why?" Zoe asked. R.L. turned to her. "Why should we trust you? We don't know you, we don't know each other. We don't even know where we are. This is shady as heck."

R.L. smiled. "You're right Zoe, and you have every reason to be cautious. Believe me when I say, I want to help you, that's why you're here. Cirque is a safe place. A place for our old selves to meet the selves we were meant to be."

Drew couldn't pinpoint the exact emotion he was feeling at the moment. It was something between confusion and curiosity.

"You're crazy," Jordan told the Ringleader.

"Rightly so." R.L. took a few steps forward. "So, is anyone interested in seeing the rest of Cirque?" The group remained silent. "Or we can sit here all night. Although, I'm sure you're all very hungry. It's been a long journey getting here."

After a tense moment, Drew got up and walked cautiously towards R.L.

"What are you doing?" Michael asked Drew in disbelief.

Drew shrugged his shoulders. "After the day I've had, I've got nothing to lose. I would guess you guys don't either."

The rest of the group shared tentative looks. Finally, Michael sighed and followed behind Drew. Zoe walked with her arms crossed and Lilly with shaking hands. Jordan walked the farthest away stomping his feet, his mind reeling trying to hatch an escape plan.

The group trailed behind R.L. as they went through a hallway with dozens of different tapestries hanging on the walls, all of them depicting people living life in a beautiful city. The floor of the hallway was a clean white and gray marble with gold specks scattered throughout. The marble made R.L.'s footsteps echo. He walked casually with his hands in his pockets, bobbing his head from side to side as if he were singing a happy song in his mind.

"So, what are we doing here exactly?" Michael asked. R.L. turned to the group smiling. Lilly gasped when she saw his eyes up close. Dancing around his brown irises were orange streaks, moving in such a way that it looked like playful flames swaying.

His voice was as warm as his eyes. "Everything will be explained in due time. I promise that you are all much safer here than you were at home." Each teenager thought about that. "I brought you here for a reason, one that will be known to you soon."

Lilly's heart ached for her family, she couldn't even imagine the grief and guilt they were experiencing right now. She just wanted to be home with them. She shuddered as she remembered the pain in her chest and her eyesight blurring. She glanced around to see if anyone noticed her reaction, but R.L. was walking straight ahead and everyone else was taking in every detail of the hallways they passed through.

"You will all be given the best treatment here." R.L. grabbed their attention. "Our guests always enjoy their stay. Anything you want or need, all you have to do is ask. Come now, we're almost there," R.L. told them.

Jordan's anxiety made him itch for anything to take the edge off.

They turned a corner and found themselves in another hallway. In this one, various picture frames lined the walls. Some were simple modern square frames and others were oval with intricate gold designs. The pictures themselves varied with age. A frame holding a group wearing bell-bottoms and fringe hung right next to an oil painting of women in long dresses and men in white wigs. In every photo, the people were smiling and standing in front of red and white stripes.

R.L. stopped walking and faced the group. "This is the Hall of Choice." He gestured to three doors on his right and three on his left.

Drew stood wide-eyed at the first door to R.L.'s right. "Pure gold," R.L. commented. Drew's mouth dropped. *No way,* he thought. "Behind that door is all you desire." Drew gave him a questioning look, but R.L. offered no further explanation.

Next to the Door of Desire was the complete opposite of the shining pure gold. The door was made of split weak wood, it was barely holding onto the hinges. It looked like it had been there forever. Through the many cracks of the door, a light was leaking. "Behind that door," R.L. spoke tenderly, "is everything you need."

Jordan stared at his reflection in a chrome door that was to the left of the Room of Need. He could see himself perfectly. There were no bruises on his face, no blood– it was like that night hadn't happened. He reached up to touch his face but quickly put his hand down and straightened up hoping no one had noticed.

"That leads to what could be. The Door of Opportunity," R.L. told him.

Officer Blight's voice echoed in Jordan's mind, *I truly believe that you have the potential to do great things.'* Jordan clenched his fists and quickly stepped away from himself.

"What's this door?" Zoe asked. She stood across from the Door of Desire in front of tall wooden double doors with black iron stretched like branches all across it. She could hear the faint playing of a slightly out of tune piano.

"The Lost Room, abandoned dreams and such," R.L. told her.

Suddenly a loud bang resounded from the scariest looking door any of them had ever seen. It stood one door over from The Lost Room. Thick black metal towered above the group with heavy chains crisscrossing it as if the multiple locks above the door handle weren't enough. A barely visible red hue was coming off of it and voices could be heard from behind it.

"Do we even want to know where that leads?" Michael asked.

"No need to worry, nothing's going in or coming out. I'm the only one with the keys to that door." R.L. flipped a rusty key chain filled with skeleton keys around his index finger. "We are going through *this* door." The last door in the hallway, between The Lost Room and The Dark Door, was a vibrant red wooden door with a large *C* painted onto it in gold. Drew recognized it as the same *C* on the back of the Contortionists' outfits. R.L. put his key ring in his pocket and turned the knob.

Conversations and music and laughter filled the ears of the group as they stood at the top of a multi-colored staircase. Hundreds of people came into view. Some were reading, some playing instruments, some throwing darts– they were all scattered around what looked like the largest living room in existence. It was filled with couches, and mismatched chairs, and rugs; some Persian, some fur, some solid colors.

Hanging from high ceilings was a collection of different lights; from huge gold chandeliers to single bulbs hanging by a wire. Lamps filled the room sitting on different tables; log and glass and metal. Four brick fireplaces blazed, filling the room with a warm glow. Statues and sculptures stood beautifully. Tapestries covered parts of the walls, while pictures, and posters, and paintings covered the rest. There wasn't a blank spot on any wall in the room. R.L. was halfway down the stairs when he realized he wasn't being followed. Each teenager was mesmerized by the sight before them. He whistled for the teenagers' attention and spoke as they walked.

"This is the Commons," he told them. Suddenly they were surrounded and practically mobbed by the performers they had seen in the circus. Everyone smiled and greeted the group as they walked through the room. The clowns, jugglers, and equestrians. The knife thrower and human cannonball. They shouted and cheered and made it seem like the whole reason they were happy was that these five strangers were now at Cirque. *Too friendly,* the teenagers thought.

"You're welcome to come here anytime. There's almost always some kind of competition happening." R.L. watched a few dart players for a moment before proceeding with the tour. "Make yourselves at home here. Find a favorite chair, a favorite corner, and just be comfortable." Zoe wondered about that. She couldn't remember the last time she was comfortable anywhere.

They walked straight through the Commons and down a hallway of stained glass murals on the walls and ceiling that depicted the circus show. Jordan looked to his right and left down all the different hallways breaking off from the one they were standing in. He was determined to get back to reality. *There has to be a way out of this place.*

At the end of the hallway was the entrance to a large bustling kitchen. High ceilings with vertical wood beams spanning the length of the room hung above a black and white tiled floor. Cooks ran amuck with produce and seasoning, following the orders of a woman whose chef's hat stood taller than she did.

"Salt," she said after tasting a spoonful of soup. "R.L.!" She bounded over to the group with her fork still in hand. "This is them?" she asked with sheer excitement. She spoke with an Irish accent and had red curly hair escaping from under her hat. The buttons on her chef's uniform were gold, and a red cursive C was stitched on each of her shoulders. She observed the teenagers causing them all to squirm.

R.L. nodded. "This is them." He put an arm around the woman, "This is Amelia, master of all that has to do with food. Anything you want, she'll whip up."

"I will!" she confirmed. Drew smiled at her excitement. She had freckles that stood out on her cheeks. Suddenly her green eyes widened with alarm and her nose sniffed furiously, "It was grand meeting all of you, we'll be thick as thieves we will, when I don't have a chicken burning!" With a smile and a wink, she scurried off to rescue the food. Lilly giggled.

After exiting the kitchen, the group turned left and a short hallway led them to a set of white French double doors that sat across from a large staircase. R.L. opened the doors to reveal a magnificent library. The bookshelves reached the ceiling and ladders stood against them waiting for an eager reader to climb. Zoe wanted nothing more than to run her fingers along the bindings of the books, pick one out, and then spend the day completely immersed in it.

"I figured you would especially enjoy this, Zoe." R.L. beamed.

"How could you have known she would like this? Have you been following us? Are you some sort of stalker? Huh? Is this a cult? Are you gonna murder us? Are we being punked?" Michael fired question after question.

Jordan crossed his arms over his chest and ground his teeth together.

R.L. took a deep breath. "Anything I say right now would sound preposterous. So, I ask that you give me time and that you give Cirque time. I promise you, sooner than you think, you will never want to leave."

Jordan chuckled dryly. "Unbelievable."

"Can you at least tell us where we are?" Michael asked.

"Yes," R.L. said. "You're with me." He smiled a brilliant smile. Jordan rolled his eyes and mumbled under his breath.

R.L. led them out of the library. "Now right up these stairs are your rooms." The group followed silently, each person more confused than before.

"Here you are ladies, Lilly and Zoe." R.L. opened a door to a small room with two beds across from each other with a trunk at the foot of each. "You'll find your clothing necessities in those trunks there. Boys you're over here." He opened a door across the hall. One bunk bed and one single bed faced each other accompanied by trunks as well.

"Your trunks also hold your garments. I'll leave you for now. Dinner is in one hour. My right hand Barnaby will come to fetch you." The teenagers just stared at him. "One thing I can tell you is"—they all leaned in, hoping to have some clarity about what was happening—"everything you know is about to change." R.L. tapped his cane on the ground twice before disappearing, leaving nothing but his wisp of red glittering smoke behind.

"Woah." Michael blinked a couple hundred times to make sure he saw right.

"This just keeps getting weirder," Drew said.

"He's real helpful." Jordan stomped into their room.

Lilly followed Zoe into their bedroom. "I call top bunk!" The girls heard Michael yell as the doors closed.

The girls' room had navy blue walls with beautiful gold detailed trim. The floor was distressed wood and there were a few colorful rugs around. There was a single large window on the wall opposite the door. In front of the window were two armchairs, one light blue, and one beige. Lilly walked over to the window and her mouth fell open at the sight.

She saw a blue sky and a turquoise body of water. Huge black figures moved beneath the waters. Her mind raced trying to imagine what kind of creatures they could be. White shores bordered the water and tall trees stood on the left side of the lake. The sun glittered making everything sparkle. It looked almost too beautiful to be real.

"Where could we be?" she said aloud. Zoe joined her at the window and gasped.

"Somewhere far away from where I live, that's for sure." Zoe looked for a moment longer and then looked back to the room.

"This one's yours." Lilly turned around as Zoe motioned to a trunk with an L carved into it in bold fancy script.

Lilly let out a sigh and sat on her bed. It had a gold frame that matched the trim of the walls. The pillows and blankets were white and the softest things she had ever felt.

"You okay?" Zoe asked as she sat on the edge of her own bed. She raised her eyebrows at the perfect feeling of the mattress.

"I don't know," Lilly answered truthfully. She crossed her legs and rested her head on her hands.

"I feel you." Zoe laid down.

The girls sat there, one staring at the ceiling and one staring at the floor. One missing home and one grateful to be away. Both wondering what was to become of them.

CHAPTER 15. MARKED

"*Z oe,*" *Paul's voice taunted her. Zoe sat in her closet trembling. She heard his footsteps getting closer and closer. She cried helplessly. "Zoe. You can't hide from me. You can never get away from me." The closet door opened and Zoe screamed. Paul pulled her out by her hair and hit her over and over again. "No!" Zoe screamed. "No! No! No!"*

Zoe gasped as she sat up and frantically looked around. Tears sprung in her eyes. *Where am I?* She wasn't home, this wasn't her room. She turned and saw a girl staring back at her—Lilly. Then she remembered everything: the circus, the Ringleader, the other teenagers, and her death. She sighed and wiped her eyes quickly.

"Are you okay?" Lilly whispered. She had watched Zoe squirm and murmur in her sleep. She had definitely been having a nightmare.

"Yeah," Zoe said unconvincingly. "Just a bad dream."

"Must've been really bad."

Zoe nodded avoiding eye contact. She wasn't about to talk about it with Lilly. The poor girl looked terrified, with her wide eyes and her knees curled up to her chest. A chime filled the room, causing both girls to look around to see where it had come from and what it could mean.

"Knock Knock!" Both bedroom doors opened to the hallway at the same time and the teenagers stared at a short man with a round belly who couldn't stand still for the life of him. He had curly light brown hair and round green eyes. In the pocket of his dark red suede vest was a gold pocket watch and in his hand was a paper filled clipboard. Drew noticed the pen tucked behind his ear and the pen in his clipboard-free hand. "Hello! Nice to meet you all, so happy to have you join us here at Cirque. That beautiful sound you just heard signifies when meals are ready. Dinner will be served momentarily, follow me!" he spoke quickly and walked even faster towards the staircase.

"I'm gonna go out on a limb here and guess that was Barnaby," Michael said as the group sped up to catch him.

"Any volunteers to push him off that limb?" mumbled Jordan.

Barnaby scurried down the stairs, to the left, past the library and through another hallway. This hallway was lined with shelves all the way down holding all sorts of different knick-knacks: ancient-looking books, snow globes with intricate scenes, fossils, compasses, and a variety of plants.

At the end of the hallway, a large marble archway welcomed the group into the dining room. Tall windows from floor to ceiling surrounded one giant table. The table had hundreds of chairs around it, a variety of different styles. It was the length of the room with other rectangle tables coming out of it at different places. Gold chandeliers hung from a mosaic ceiling of red and white stripes.

"What kind of table—" Michael let his sentence hang along with his mouth as he stared amazed at the room.

"You can sit right over here." Barnaby brought them towards a table in the front of the room. The group sat down and within a few seconds, they were joined by a man and woman who Lilly recognized as two of the Tightrope Walkers.

"Hiya!" the woman said.

"Heya!" the man said. Their blue eyes dazzled and their blonde hair shined. They had matching pointed noses and high cheekbones.

"I'm Mia!"

"I'm Milo!" They shook hands with everyone and sat down once they went over everyone's names three times. "We wouldn't want to forget," Mia said. "That would be embarrassing," followed Milo.

A woman sat down next to Zoe. Her dark brown hair was styled in a pixie cut and she had a small scar running through the right side of her lips. "I'm Abrielle."

"You're the girl they stuffed in a box," Michael said.

Abrielle laughed and nodded. "It's not as cramped as it looks."

"Really?" Drew asked.

"I'm lying, it totally is. I've learned how to hold my breath." She laughed loudly and the teenagers chuckled, none of them completely comfortable yet.

"So what do you guys think of Cirque so far?" Milo asked.

"I think you're all crazy," Jordan told him bluntly.

The twins laughed.

"You're right," Abrielle told him with a smile. "But there's something you don't realize."

"And what's that?" Jordan asked tightly.

Abrielle put her arms on the table, leaned forward, looked at everyone, and whispered, "You're all crazy, too." Jordan furrowed his eyebrows and Abrielle just chuckled.

"Ooh! R.L.'s here!" Mia excitedly faced the front of the room, everyone followed suit.

"Good evening my fellow freaks!" R.L. greeted the room. Hoops and hollers resounded throughout the dining hall. People banged on the table and stomped on the ground. R.L. joined them with a loud shout, "Let's raise a toast!" Everyone stood and lifted their glasses in the air. "Tonight's dinner is not only to celebrate another successful show but also to honor and celebrate the arrival of our guests. Cirque, let us welcome the newest members of our family—Lilly, Jordan, Zoe, Drew, and Michael."

Everyone cheered as they eagerly surveyed the group. Lilly shifted uncomfortably from all the attention, Jordan stared at his hands, Zoe burned holes into the table with her eyes, Drew meekly glanced at those around him, and Michael stood up, smiled and waved.

R.L. laughed a booming, infectious laugh that filled the dining hall. He then announced, "Let us feast!"

Servers in white shirts and red bow ties came out of swinging doors carrying trays of every food imaginable. Classical music filled the room, though Lilly couldn't find where it was coming from. Michael tried not to stare at some of the people sitting at the surrounding tables. He saw a woman covered in hair and a whole family covered in green scales. There was even a man who was so tiny he had to sit on the actual table and eat from a plate that was the size of Michael's palm.

"They're the Side Show performers," Milo told him.

"Side Show?" Michael asked.

"The show before the show. People see them first and then come see us."

Michael nodded understanding. They were the *real* freaks.

Conversation hummed as forks clanged against plates and glasses were set down on tables. Lilly ate some vegetables and bread, but she lacked any real appetite. This was so much to take in at once. Jordan just stared angrily at the food, not wanting to take anything from these people.

"So have you guys been Marked yet?" Mia asked as she stabbed a meatball with her fork.

"Have we been what?" Drew questioned.

"Marked. You'll receive a mark that shows you what you're going to be. You're chosen to either be a Fire Breather, Tightrope Walker, Contortionist, and so on," Mia rambled.

"No, we haven't. We didn't know," Drew told the twins.

"It will probably happen tonight and you'll begin training tomorrow." Abrielle stuffed a forkful of salad in her mouth. Lilly looked worriedly at Zoe.

"Training?" Lilly whispered. "I don't train."

"I'm sure they're just joking. We'll be fine," Zoe told her, trying not to show her own nervousness.

"That Ringleader's delusional if he thinks I'm going to become a circus freak." Jordan shuddered at the thought of wearing a leotard and prancing around in front of hundreds of people.

Zoe just picked at her food, not being able to shake away the nightmare she had about Paul and now the prospect of having to work with these people to join their circus— her head was starting to hurt.

"Not hungry?" Abrielle asked her. Zoe shook her head. "You really will grow to love Cirque." Abrielle smiled softly as she spoke.

"How are you so sure?" Zoe asked.

"It's impossible not to," Abrielle said.

A bell rang and the waiters came and traded the dinner plates with dessert. Every type of sweet food was placed in front of Michael. He didn't know what to do with himself. Zoe wrinkled her nose in distaste as Michael took a bite of blueberry pie, then three-layer chocolate cake, and then apple fritter, followed by a chunk of cheesecake. The waiters came out again and cleared all the dishes. Everyone stood up and cheered and clapped for the waiters. The staff took their bows and then turned to go into the kitchen.

"It was so nice having dinner with you all!" Mia smiled as she pushed her chair in.

"We'll see you in training tomorrow!" Milo held out his arm for his sister to take and they skipped out of the dining room.

"Good luck tonight, guys." Abrielle smiled and waved goodbye. The group sat back down trying to digest everything they had just eaten and heard. The dining room began to clear out but some people still sat and talked.

"This is so weird," Lilly whispered.

"It can't be real," Jordan responded. He leaned back in his chair with his arms crossed. "It's not real."

"What if it is?" Michael asked.

"It's not!" Jordan said harshly.

There was no more talking after that until R.L. came and took a seat at the table next to Lilly. "Did you enjoy dinner?" he asked. The group nodded. "I see you especially did Michael." R.L. laughed as he wiped the side of his own mouth to convey the message to Michael. Michael quickly wiped the crumbs off with the back of his hand.

"Mia and Milo mentioned something about being Marked?" Drew asked R.L.

"Yes, it is where we're going now. The trade you are meant for will be revealed tonight."

"What are we going to have to do?" Lilly asked while her hands played with the hem of her sweater.

"You will train in whatever art your Markings show for."

"You make it sound so easy." Zoe's knee bounced nervously.

"It's easier than you think. Whatever is revealed is what you are destined for. It will come naturally to you all." They stared at him in disbelief. "Trust me." Jordan laughed at that, but R.L. just smiled. "Follow me please."

They left the dining room and somehow, after going through a couple of hallways, ended up in the Commons. Instead of going towards the staircase they descended down earlier, they took a left and walked down a dimly lit hallway. R.L. opened a door to their right revealing Barnaby holding his clipboard close. The room was dark apart from the few candles that hung on the gray stone walls. A white stone podium stood in the center of the room and there was a hatch in the ceiling above it.

"Here." Barnaby took Drew and Zoe and placed them to the right of the podium. Lilly and Jordan stood to the left and Michael stood behind the podium facing Barnaby who now stood near the door.

"This will not hurt you, you will feel a slight tingle but it is harmless." Michael opened his mouth to ask a question. "Shh," R.L. told him as he pulled down a lever that opened the hatch.

A breeze blew quickly into the room and a single beam of moonlight hit the podium and then reflected off into five more beams. Everyone held their breath as the light hit each teenager in the base of their neck and disappeared into their skin.

"Woah." Drew was in awe as he watched the bright light shoot down both of his arms. On every left arm, a tingling sensation caused them to crease their eyebrows. Each watched as the moonlight revealed a tattoo on the skin of their inner forearm. A tattoo determining their trade.

"My mom is gonna kill me," Lilly said. She traced the art on her arm. A figure was outlined that stood atop the black line that stretched across her skin.

"Tightrope Walker," R.L. told her as he looked over her shoulder. "Fire Breather," He told Jordan. A figure holding a torch of flames showed on his arm.

"Contortionist?" Zoe asked as she held her arm out. R.L. nodded at the bent human inked into it.

"Lion Tamer." Drew gawked at the inked person and lion that occupied his skin.

Michael's arm showed an acrobat hanging upside down on a trapeze bar. "And I'm supposed to swing like a monkey in a leotard."

"Shouldn't be too hard," Jordan told him.

"It is a noble trade, Michael." R.L. patted him on the back. He walked to the middle of the room. "Congratulations." R.L. smiled proudly. "You've all been Marked. You've been chosen."

"And you expect us to learn how to do all this stuff?" Drew asked.

"No," R.L. said as he took away the moonlight when he closed the hatch. "I expect you to master it."

Barnaby smiled to himself when he heard several gulps of nervousness. He opened the door and the group piled out of the room.

"R.L.?" Lilly said as they walked back towards their rooms. It had taken her several minutes to work up the courage to speak. Her voice cracked and she stared at her shoes. R.L. turned to her.

"I, I just," she took a deep breath. "I just don't understand." Everyone was silent to try to hear her quiet voice. "How are we here?" Lilly couldn't shake the memories of leaning against her front door while her body failed her.

"I brought you here," he told her gently.

"But how?" her voice was louder now with desperation. She lowered it again to almost a whisper, "I mean the last thing I remember I was—" she stopped herself when she noticed everyone listening. She didn't want to announce to them all how she had been destroying herself.

"Go on Lilly, it's okay," R.L. urged her to continue.

"I just don't understand how I'm here. How I'm okay," she spoke quickly and looked intently at the floor.

Michael cleared his throat and looked to his right at the wall. "I'm with her on that one. Last thing I remember I was roadkill thanks to a four-door piece of crap." He scratched behind his ear and continued to avoid eye contact.

Lilly's head whipped around in astonishment. "Really?"

Michael looked at her and nodded. It was silent for a moment.

"I remember dying, too," Drew said. "I killed myself, I um, I swallowed pills." He coughed out the lump in his throat.

Jordan subconsciously touched his stomach, almost remembering the pain. The group looked at him expectantly. "I was stabbed." He shrugged as if it had been nothing.

Everyone looked at Zoe. Her eyes widened realizing they wanted to know her story. "Oh, uh, my, uh, my stepfather killed me, or at least I, I thought he had." She cracked her knuckles nervously.

"I died, too, I was starving myself. I mean, I guess I didn't die, but I should've. I thought I did," Lilly confessed.

"How is this possible?" Drew looked at R.L. "We all remember what we thought was our last moments. How are we standing here with you right now? Did we die? Is this an afterlife?"

R.L. seemed to be finding the right words to say in response. He looked at Barnaby who was behind the group and then looked back at them.

"I can't explain to you how you are here but I can tell you why." R.L. took a step closer. None of the teenagers realized it, but they each leaned in towards him. "This is a second chance. Those markings"—he grabbed his own coat covered arm—"that is your identity. An identity you never knew you had. As you learn your trades you will come to realize exactly what it means to be a Lion Tamer, a Contortionist, a Trapeze Artist, a Fire Breather and a Tightrope Walker. Think of Cirque as an opportunity to start over and see yourselves from a brand new angle."

His words echoed in their thoughts as they all crawled to bed that night exhausted.

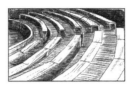

CHAPTER 16. BORN FOR THIS

D rew slouched in the leather armchair in his room and looked out the window to beautiful mountain scenery. He had gone skiing with his parents once when he was very young. He wasn't good at it and ended up spraining his ankle. His mom spent the entire time in the lodge drinking spiked hot chocolate and his dad was frustrated with every little thing from the service, to the food, to the snow. Drew hadn't been to the mountains again, but the ones he looked at now were different. They were serene, untouched. They looked so perfect, so fragile even though they towered high into the sky.

"I wonder if breakfast is ready." Michael sat up from where he lay on his bed.

Jordan sat on the floor, leaning against his bed with his legs stretched out in front of him, facing the door. He hadn't spoken a word all morning, just dirty looks and annoyed grunts.

Suddenly the chime for breakfast sounded and Michael jumped off of his top bunk. They met the girls in the hallway and headed towards the dining room. Jordan walked a couple of feet behind everyone else.

"I had the best sleep of my life last night," Michael said. Zoe nodded in agreement.

"The beds are so comfy." Lilly played with her long sleeves.

"Does anyone else still think they're dreaming?" Drew asked, receiving nods and yeses.

"Morning!" R.L. greeted the group as they walked into the dining hall for breakfast. Some smiled, some just nodded blankly and Jordan didn't even acknowledge him. R.L. knew their minds were still trying to grasp the fact that this was all really happening and he was allowing them their time and space. He knew the drill.

They sat down and started filling their plates. R.L. sat next to Drew who gave him a small smile. Jordan looked just as angry as the day before, Lilly still looked a bit sad. Zoe shifted uncomfortably as she sat next to Michael and she scooted a little closer to Lilly. No one seemed to notice except R.L.

R.L. smiled. "After you finish your breakfast I would like to introduce you all to your trainers. We'll all go to the circus ring and get started."

"You were serious about that?" Zoe asked.

"Very," R.L. said.

"No," Jordan didn't look at R.L. when he spoke. The table looked at him with uneasiness.

"No to training?" R.L. didn't seem offended, only interested.

"Of course not!" Jordan looked at the Ringleader in the face now. "I don't know what's going on here but you can't make me train to be some act in your stupid circus. It's the dumbest thing I've ever heard, doesn't even make sense!" his loud voice earned him the attention of several people sitting around them. They gave looks of sympathy, of understanding, and even a few of slight amusement, like they knew something the rest of them didn't.

"I think you'll change your mind, Jordan."

"Yeah? And what? You just think you know everything?"

"Yes," R.L. answered sincerely.

Michael chuckled.

The group just marveled at the Ringleader. Zoe tried to remind herself that this man was a stranger, but she wanted to wrap herself in every word he said. He felt safe, friendly, warm. *No*, she told herself mentally. *Approach with caution.* She looked away and back to Jordan.

"Well, you don't. I'm not training." He folded his arms.

"Okay." Jordan was surprised at R.L.'s response.

"What?" Jordan asked.

"If you wish to not train that's fine. I don't force anyone to do anything. You have to come to it on your own. Everything here is a choice," R.L. told him.

"Yeah, exactly," Jordan said in an unsure tone.

"Hey, gang." Abrielle smiled as she passed by. The group waved and continued eating their breakfast.

"Have you been sleeping well?" R.L. asked. Everyone nodded slightly, even Zoe who was still having nightmares about Paul.

"That's good. Sometimes a few people have recurring nightmares of something that might have happened to them before arriving here. It's completely normal if you are," R.L. knew he was speaking to Zoe, but he didn't look at her. "If any of you do experience that I can be of assistance. A sleep-deprived performer is no good to the circus." Zoe stared at her plate.

"R.L." Barnaby came to the table and greeted the group. "Can I borrow you for a moment?"

"Of course." R.L. stood. "Excuse me," he said to the table. They watched the two walk out of the dining hall and into a crowd of noisy clowns before disappearing from view.

"It's going to be interesting to see what this 'training' will be like," Michael said with air quotes. No one responded to him. Drew just slightly nodded.

"So where are you all from?" Michael asked as he cut a piece of pancake. Everyone looked at him confused. "What? We're stuck here, might as well not be total strangers." One by one they each revealed their home city, Jordan being the last and most reluctant.

"Wow," Drew said amazed at the different places everyone was from. None of them lived anywhere near each other.

"It really makes you wonder how we all got here," Lilly said.

"And where exactly *here* is," Drew said.

"I never did believe in an afterlife," Michael spoke. The waiters came around and began clearing dishes. R.L. returned to the dining room.

"Are you ready?" he asked the group. He could feel them all tense up with nerves. "Jordan feel free to roam wherever you please. If you change your mind about training, we will be in the circus ring. If you get lost ask anyone and they'll be glad to direct you." Jordan nodded curtly.

"Alright, let's get to it!" R.L. tossed his cane in the air and caught it while turning from the group, leading them out of the dining hall. They walked to the Commons and Jordan stayed put in the middle of the room as he watched the group go up the stairs and through the red door. He had no idea what to do or where to go, but he was determined to find a way out.

The group followed R.L. into the circus ring. Several people were in the room and they all turned to see the newest additions to their acts. The teenagers gulped nervously as they looked at the performers. They all wore normal clothing and smiled sincerely, but the expectation of having to do what they do was overwhelming.

Milo and Mia were on the other side of the ring warming up, but they hollered everyone's names as soon as they spotted them. R.L. and the teenagers stopped in front of a group of five people, Abrielle being one of them. She smiled happily. The people who stood next to Abrielle were all so different. To her right, a tall muscular man with broad shoulders and a thick beard stood in a black vest and a black leotard that left his legs covered and arms bare.

"You have already met Abrielle. She is a master Contortionist and will be training you, Zoe. This is Alfie, a rope walker like no other," R.L. said with a kind smile directed at him. "He will be training you, Lilly. And lovely Annette will be training Jordan as a Fire Breather."

"He didn't show?" Annette, an elderly woman with gray hair up in a bun and dark red painted lips, asked. She raised an eyebrow and tilted her head. She wore a leather vest, with various patches sewn on, over a black long-sleeved shirt.

"Not yet but he'll come around," he assured her. Annette just rolled her eyes and sucked her teeth. The group grinned at that.

R.L. continued introducing two men to Anette's right. "Drew, this is Wyatt, our youngest master of the lions. He will be your instructor." Wyatt had a youthful glow on him. His brown hair was wild and curly. He smiled wide and the teenagers noticed a couple of silver crowns in his mouth. Next to him was a well-built very serious-looking man. He stood at a shorter than average height but held his head high and shoulders back. "And this is Dez, truly an impeccable artist, he will be training you, Michael, on the trapeze."

R.L. stepped in front of the teenagers to face them. "They have all been eager to meet you and train with you. Trust them. They are here to help. You were made to do specifically each of these things, remind yourself of that until you believe it." He turned to the trainers and gave them a respectful nod.

"Let's go!" Abrielle excitedly dragged Zoe away to the far side of the room.

"Hello, Lilly. At your service." Alfie bowed and grinned causing Lilly's frown to slowly morph into a small smile. *Maybe this won't be too bad,* she thought.

"Michael, it is an honor to train you. Follow me." Dez turned and walked quickly causing Michael to practically run in an attempt to catch up.

"Hey." Wyatt and Drew shook hands. "It's nice to meet you. Before we get started, there's something you need to see." The two walked away through the giant curtains into a large room with several hallways connecting it.

"Where is he?" Annette asked R.L.

"Wandering about."

"I'll find him," Anette said with an eye-roll.

"He'll find you first," R.L. said.

"How are you so sure?"

"He's eager for something, he just doesn't know what it is. He'll soon figure out it is a purpose. Then he will come straight here."

She huffed, "Fine. You're too nice sometimes, you know that? And why is it that my recruits are always the troublemakers, huh? You do that on purpose?"

"They're always just like you used to be." R.L. smiled and Annette gave him a playful push.

"So, let's get started with some simple stretches." Abrielle rolled out two yoga mats and sat down on one, encouraging Zoe to do the same. Abrielle instructed Zoe to stretch her legs out in front of her and try to reach her toes.

"Man, talk about Karma. This is what I get for always skipping gym class."

"You're doing great!" Abrielle encouraged as she attempted to push Zoe further towards her toes. Zoe let out a grunt and mumbled her grievances out of earshot. "It'll all get easier over time. Soon you'll be able to do this." Abrielle brought her legs up and behind her head. Zoe groaned and lay sprawled out on the floor.

Wyatt had told Drew he was bringing him to meet Tyran, the lion that he had seen in the circus. Drew had never been up close to a lion before and didn't have any plans to change that. He still couldn't believe he was following this stranger through a circus. They entered a hallway with a myriad of colored doors.

"Each opens to a different animal habitat," Wyatt explained. He gestured to one of the doors on his right. "Through here you're in the plains of India and you'll see Brutus and the other elephants." He pointed to another door. "Through this one, you're in the American west on thousands of beautiful acres where our Stallions roam. Tyran is this way."

Wyatt opened an orange door towards the end of the hallway. Stepping through the door, Drew stood on grass and overlooked a never-ending wilderness landscape. The sun assaulted him, he wiped the sweat from his forehead. Wyatt began walking and Drew numbly followed. "Where are we?" he asked in shock.

"Tyran's land," Wyatt answered like it was obvious. As if they weren't standing in what looked like African plains. As they neared a watering hole, Wyatt put his hand out to stop Drew. They stood staring at a bundle of rocks occupied by a pride of lions. "There's so many," Drew observed.

"Well, we're not gonna leave old Tyran by himself."

"Oh," was all Drew could mutter.

Wyatt whistled loudly catching the attention of the king who laid upon the highest point of the rocks. Tyran stood up, looked over at the Lion Tamers and made his way forward. He walked slowly but proudly, making it clear that this was his domain and Drew and Wyatt were only guests. Tyran stood a few feet from the tamers and Wyatt bowed his head in respect. Drew, though absolutely terrified, did the same.

They lifted their heads and Wyatt instructed Drew, "Go to him slowly, kneel down on one knee and look him in the eyes. After a moment he will take a step back and then you will walk back over to me. You must establish yourself to him."

Drew shook his head. "No way. I'm not gonna stand within the gnawing distance of a lion."

"You will," Wyatt said confidently.

"Nope." Drew looked at Tyran. "Definitely not."

"Drew." Wyatt turned to face the tamer in training. "This is what you were destined for. You can do this. There's no need to be afraid." Wyatt nudged him forward.

Drew let out an uneasy breath and started towards the lion. He followed Wyatt's instructions precisely. Drew looked into Tyran's eyes and fear was no longer the strongest emotion. Determination took its place. It was a new feeling—a passionate excitement Drew had never experienced before. It was like every fiber of his being was pushing him to face the lion and win. He stared into the eyes of the king of the jungle, and then the king took a step back. Drew stood and returned to Wyatt. The tamers bowed their heads once more.

"Now, Tyran won't be the lion you'll be working with," Wyatt told him.

"What? Why?"

"You have to face your own lion." Wyatt let out a whistle and another lion laying in the sun looked up. He walked slowly to the Lion Tamers, "This is Asier, *your* lion. Do the same thing you did with Tyran."

Drew did as instructed.

Asier didn't step back as quickly as Tyran had done. "What's wrong?" Drew whispered to Wyatt.

"You're Asier's first trainer. He's not used to this yet. Stand your ground."

"What? Are you kidding me?" he exclaimed in a whisper. "He could kill me!"

"Drew, you got this."

Drew remained kneeling and staring into Asier's eyes with challenging ones of his own. Finally, Asier took a step back. Drew stood to his feet and practically ran away when Asier let out a ground-shaking roar.

"Enough!" Wyatt yelled. The lion returned to his pride.

Once they were back in the hallway Drew couldn't contain himself. "That was crazy!" he rasped as he slumped against the wall.

Wyatt laughed. "What did I tell ya'?"

Drew straightened. "It was like this confidence suddenly overtook me. I felt like I could actually do it."

"Because this is what you were meant to do."

"Crazy. Asier needs some work though," Drew whispered. *And I have to be the one to do it, this is insane.*

Wyatt chuckled as they walked towards the circus ring.

"Now we move onto to the other elements of training."

"What are they?"

"Just simple strength building and teaching you how to combat a lion."

"Oh, is that all?" Wyatt laughed again and Drew's stomach tangled up with nerves.

"I can't," Lilly whispered to Alfie. She shook her head and hugged her body.

Soft music filtered through the circus ring as Lilly stood in front of a four-foot-high gymnastics beam.

"Trust me, Lilly. I have been doing this for a very, very long time," Alfie spoke in his thick accent.

"I'm gonna fall." Lilly's palms clammed up.

"You will if you make yourself believe it."

"It's only my first day!" she squeaked.

"Lilly, I am right here. I never let any of my students hit the ground, you may fall yes, but I am here for you. You were *made* for this."

Lilly took a deep breath and willed her breakfast to stay in her stomach.

She stepped up to the beam and Alfie held on to her hand as she placed one foot in front of the other.

Alfie spoke as she walked, "Step one is to get rid of any fear of heights you may have. Walk. Deep breaths." She took one step and used her free hand to wipe her eyes where her tears had begun to form. "Just one step at a time, Lilly. One step at a time."

She took two more steps. "Amazing," Alfie encouraged. With each step, he spoke words to lift her spirits. "You are a natural. Good job. Fantastic." She made it to the other side and Mia and Milo clapped excitedly.

Lilly smiled widely and caught her breath. She couldn't believe she made it all the way across.

"Now turn around and walk back." Her nerves peaked again. She opened her mouth to argue with Alfie but the smile on his face and the confidence in his eyes settled her anxieties a bit.

Alfie helped her find her balance and turn around on the beam. She took a deep breath and started back, much quicker than the first time. She squeezed Alfie's hand in excitement.

"Now turn around again and go back." Lilly turned around more confidently and walked to the other end in record time. "You didn't even notice," Alfie spoke.

"Notice what?" Lilly looked to her right but there was no one there. She turned around on the beam and stared with her mouth open at Alfie who was on the other side.

"You did it by yourself."

Her eyes widened. *No way.*

Alfie laughed, causing her to laugh. She saw the pride in Alfie's eyes, the smiles on Milo and Mia's faces. She felt like she had known them all her life.

The group sat together in the dining hall recounting their first day of training.

"I have never been in so much pain," Zoe said and then remembered lying at the foot of the staircase with her mother desperately calling her name. She swallowed the lump in her throat.

"You?" Michael exclaimed. "I had to do actual exercise, you were just doing yoga." He waved his hand dismissively.

"I'd like to see you bend into some unnatural human pretzel." She giggled at her own comment causing Michael to do the same.

"I'd like to see both of you stand like a thousand feet above the ground and be expected to walk from one end of the circus to the other on a super-thin almost non-existent rope!" Lilly exaggerated. It was the loudest any of them had heard her talk.

"You win." Michael smiled at her as he put his hands up in surrender. Zoe nodded in agreement and laughed.

Dinner disappeared into mouths just as quick as it had appeared on the table.

"A real lion? Face-to-face?" Jordan asked Drew again. He was having a hard time believing Drew's story about Asier.

"I swear. It was like we walked through a door into Africa, like right into the *Lion King*. It was insane."

Jordan went silent again lost in his thoughts.

"Where did you go today?" Drew asked Jordan.

"Nowhere special. I walked around trying to find a way out. Then I took a nap."

"Riveting," Michael mocked in a silly accent. Lilly laughed.

"I wonder why we have to train? Like, what's the point of each of our trades?" Drew said to the group before Jordan could retort to Michael's comment. He had had enough of their arguing the night before in the bedroom.

"Something to keep us busy so we don't destroy the circus, or find out its deep dark secrets," Michael said as he got up from the table and started to leave.

"Where are you going?" Drew asked.

"To explore, maybe find some of those secrets." Michael waited at the door for the group. "Come on."

"It might be cool to see what else is here. Maybe," Lilly said softly.

Drew agreed and within a few minutes, they were all in the Hall of Choice, even Jordan who stayed a couple of feet away from the rest. He might as well learn his way around. *There's got to be an exit somewhere,* he thought to himself. Each teenager made sure to stand a safe distance from the black chained door.

"What door is this again?" Michael asked.

"The Lost Room I think," Lilly told him.

"Cool." Before anyone could say anything, he swung the ancient doors open.

The out of tune piano Lilly heard before filled the room. Dozens of broken clocks ticked in competition with each other. Chandeliers of all different styles and sizes hung from the ceiling lighting up every corner of the cluttered room. There were shelves filled with forgotten childhood books and barely written diaries and notebooks.

Half-finished paintings sat on easels and on the floor in corners. There were record players dressed in dust, cassettes lying lonely and CD players sitting untouched. The walls were covered with patches of hundreds of different wallpapers. The room was narrow and long, the only way to walk was in a single file line.

"Ow." Drew rubbed his knee and pushed aside the red tricycle he had run into.

Lilly looked at a family photo that hung on the wall. Her heart ached terribly for her parents and her sister. She felt her eyes start to water and looked to the ground in an attempt not to cry.

"This place is creepy," Zoe said to herself as she gently pushed a creaky rocking chair covered with a quilt with her foot. Everywhere she looked she made eye contact with the glassy stares of dolls.

Michael stood as tall as his tiptoes would allow and as far as he could see there was just stuff, no end to the Lost Room.

Lilly turned a corner and screamed. The rest of the group caught up to her side instantly.

"I didn't mean to startle you, I'm sorry Lilly," R.L. said.

"It's okay," she said as her heartbeat returned to normal.

"I see you guys decided to explore." R.L. looked around the room and a sad glint

formed in his eyes.

"Sorry," Lilly sheepishly apologized.

"Nothing to be sorry about. Cirque is meant to be explored. You have every right to go wherever you please."

"Where did all this stuff come from?" Michael asked. Drew stared at a beautiful oil painting that was only half-finished.

"Children who grew up. Adults that gave up," R.L. told them. "This is where the things we let go of end up. Dreams, plans, memories, everything." He reached out to a small silent clock. He opened the latch on the back of the clock and messed around with the mechanics. The clock began to tick and R.L. smiled. "There." He set the clock down and stared at it a moment more. "See? Easily fixed." R.L. turned to leave and the group followed.

Zoe took one last look at the clock R.L. had fixed. It steadily ticked, it did what it was meant to do. There was no way to tell that it had once been broken.

It was good as new.

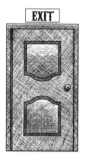

CHAPTER 17. A WAY OUT

Ll was quiet throughout the circus. Everyone was nestled in bed, even the Side Show was silent with sleep.

"Jordan? What are you doing?" Drew questioned groggily. Jordan's shuffling around the room had woken him up.

"Getting the hell out of here." Jordan tied his boots up.

Drew was wide awake now, "What?"

"You heard me. This place is creepy. We don't know where we are, how we got

here or who any of these freaks are. I'm not gonna train to be a part of a circus, this is bull. I'm smarter than that to stay here like an idiot."

"But—"

"Nah, I'm leaving." Jordan shrugged a jacket on. "You can come with," he offered.

Drew looked puzzled. Jordan was everything Drew wasn't. Strong, fearless, defiant, kinda good looking. Why would someone like that pay any attention to someone like Drew? It was flattering to be noticed, to be invited. *Maybe Jordan...no, there's no way.* Still, it was a very tempting offer, one Drew had never had before.

Drew shook his head. "I, I like it here," he said hesitantly, surprising himself with his confession.

Jordan scoffed at that, "Whatever." He went to the door.

"You're not gonna ask me to escape with you?" Michael, now awake, asked sarcastically.

"You're lucky I'm leaving, otherwise I would've knocked your perfect snotty teeth out soon."

"I'm gonna miss you so much," Michael mockingly choked up his voice.

Jordan pulled the bedroom door open and closed it behind him, careful not to let it slam.

"Now," he whispered to himself. "How do I get out of here?"

He crept warily through the Commons, almost crawled up the staircase and basically tiptoed down the hall of choice, retracing his steps from when they first arrived. His hands were slightly shaking. He clenched and unclenched his fists attempting to make them stop.

He didn't know why he was so nervous. He wanted to go home; he needed to go home. Who knows what his mom was going through. With Jordan not there to stand between her and his dad, anything could be happening. Blight was probably furious with him too for just vanishing like that, and no doubt Will thought Jordan was still pissed at him for the fight.

Jordan went through the opening in the red and white curtains and found himself in the middle of the circus ring. He shook his head. "Crazy weirdos," he muttered.

He ignored the feeling that surrounded him at the circus, almost like it was a place to belong, a safe place. He tried to shake away the image of R.L. passionately telling them that they had some great purpose to serve. He had almost let himself believe all of that crap, the idea that he was more than a dumb kid destined for trouble. It was tempting but stupid, to believe that he had some great role to play in the universe. Jordan was calling bs on all of it.

"Come on," he grumbled as he looked for an opening in the curtains. Finally, he found a door with a wooden sign that read, *EXIT*.

"Jordan," R.L. stood a few feet behind with his hands in his pockets. Jordan groaned.

"So close," he whispered.

R.L. was dressed impeccably in a dark red velvet trench coat, his hair was tucked behind his ears and the flames in his eyes glowed brightly in the dimly lit arena.

"Leaving already?" There was no anger in his eyes like Jordan had expected. Instead, there was amusement.

"I was trying to."

"Well, you found the door."

Jordan side glanced at the plain white door. *He's got to be kidding*, he shook his head, "That's it? That's the way out of this place?"

R.L. nodded, "That's the way back."

Jordan didn't know what he was expecting, but it sure wasn't an ordinary door to stand between Cirque and the real world.

"Aren't you going to tell me to go back to my room and never try to leave again?"

R.L. shook his head. "You have a choice Jordan, everyone has a choice. If you really want to, you can walk right out of that door and never have to think about Cirque again." R.L.'s eyes saddened as he told him this.

"Really?"

"Yes, really."

Jordan reached out and wrapped his hand around the brass doorknob.

"But—"

"Ah, there it is." He knew there had to be a catch.

"It would be best for you if you stayed." R.L. took a couple of steps forward.

"Why?" Jordan humored him, uninterested in what R.L.'s reasoning would be.

"Because if you walk through that door, you walk right back into your old life."

A flashback of the bar and the alley and the broken city flooded Jordan's mind.

R.L. continued, "A life where you were miserable and angry. A life where each day your resentment grew and grew," R.L. was stepping closer and closer with each word, "a life where you were living in circles, never getting out of a terrible cycle. You have a chance to change that Jordan. You have a chance to have a better life, to be a better man."

"By staying here in a freaking circus tent?" Jordan yelled. His voice echoed through the empty tent.

"Yes," R.L. said calmly.

"I don't get it," Jordan muttered. He ran his hand over his face.

"You don't believe that you're any better than your father. Is that right?" The look in Jordan's eyes was enough of an affirmative answer. "Cirque will prove you wrong. You will prove yourself wrong if you give it a chance. Please, give me a chance, but most importantly, please give yourself a chance."

Jordan looked to the door once more. He took a step, and then another.

"That's all you've got?" Dez asked Michael.

"That was like seventy-five push-ups." Michael stood rubbing his sore biceps.

"*Twenty-five* actually," Dez retorted.

Michael groaned.

"The only way you will achieve the trapeze is if you build strength in your arms. Right now you have none," his instructor told him.

"Thanks." Michael rolled his eyes.

"That was not a compliment," Dez said.

"Sarcasm," Michael said.

"Seventy-five jumping jacks. Go. Not sarcasm."

Michael grumbled under his breath as he reluctantly followed instructions.

"Here." Wyatt tossed a sword at Drew. Drew quickly sidestepped letting the sword fly past him. "You were supposed to catch it," Wyatt teased.

"We're sword fighting?"

"Fencing," Wyatt corrected.

"I don't fence," Drew said.

"You will by the end of today." Wyatt smiled and handed Drew a white helmet as he said, "Go get the sword and put this on."

Drew clamored for the sword and put his helmet on. Wyatt lunged towards Drew and he jumped back and dropped the sword.

"Try to keep the sword in your hand." Wyatt laughed.

"Right." Drew picked it up again and held it tight. Wyatt lunged again and Drew lifted up the sword on instinct blocking Wyatt's advance.

"Great!"

Drew looked at the sword in amazement. "Cool."

Drew mimicked Wyatt's footing as they fenced. "Why exactly are we fencing? I'm pretty sure Tyran isn't going to pull a sword out of his pocket to fight me with. Ouch." He stumbled and fell. Wyatt reached out and helped him up.

"The art of being a Lion Tamer is in your footing. You have to learn to be quick and purposeful with where you place your feet, just like in fencing." Wyatt then took three steps forward and unarmed Drew in a single motion. "Soon you'll be able to do that."

"Yeah, right."

"Trust me. Come on, let's go again."

R.L. watched from his office as his future circus freaks trained. He leaned against the large circular window that overlooked the circus ring. It sat high up in the tent, hidden so the audience wouldn't notice it during a show.

"They're really coming along," Barnaby commented as he came up behind R.L.

"Yes, they are. Our trainers have their work cut out for them though."

"There have been slight breaches in security." Barnaby turned his pocket watch over and over in his hand.

"Instruct The General to double the locks on everything and triple the rounds of security. We cannot let them get close to our new recruits."

"Right away." Barnaby hurried off. R.L. chuckled and shook his head at Zoe who sat with her arms crossed refusing to follow Abrielle's instructions.

Michael walked over to where Jordan was taking his break. He sat on the bleachers with a cup of water in his hand. "So decided to stay huh?" Michael asked.

"Duh." Jordan deadpanned.

"Couldn't find the way out?"

"I found it."

"Then why are you here?" Michael pestered, annoyed at Jordan's continued presence.

Jordan stood and stepped close to Michael. "To make your life hell."

"Please, my life has been hell for a while."

"Yeah, having all that money must've sucked."

"Don't act like you know me." *I can probably take him,* Michael thought to himself. He looked at Jordan again and the faint scars that seemed to be all over him. *Maybe not.*

"Don't act like I couldn't kick your—"

"Jordan," Annette called. Jordan looked at her then back at Michael.

"Whatever." Jordan tossed his empty paper cup at Michael's feet and then stomped off. He walked to the bleachers on the other side of the tent and sat down bouncing his knee in frustration. Annette walked over and sat down next to him.

"What's going on?" she asked.

"Why should I tell you?" he said angrily.

Annette just looked at him and laughed loudly. Jordan furrowed his eyebrows. She kept laughing like what he said was the funniest thing in the world. Anybody else would've gotten angry or embarrassed by the way he spoke.

She caught her breath and looked at him like he didn't phase her. "Whether you like it or not, you're stuck with me." She nudged his shoulder. "You think you're tough? Get out there, light a torch on fire, and prove it."

Jordan couldn't back down from a challenge. He ground his teeth and stood up, "Fine."

"This hurts!" Zoe whined to Abrielle.

"Eventually it won't."

"Well right now it does." Zoe began to untangle herself.

"No!" Abrielle held her in place.

"I'm sore," Zoe pleaded.

"Don't make a decision based on temporary feelings." Abrielle's hold was firm but gentle. "The more you work yourself the better you'll be. Feelings come and go but the results of hard work, no matter how hard, stay forever. Just breathe and endure. You can do this." Zoe took a deep breath. *Breathe and endure. Breathe and endure.*

"Lilly?" Alfie called to her. Her mind was elsewhere as she stared into oblivion. He gently touched her shoulder and said her name once more.

"Huh?" She looked at him. "Oh, I'm sorry."

"It's okay. What had you thinking so hard?"

Lilly shifted her weight from her right foot to her left. "I miss my family," her voice cracked. She looked to the floor. Alfie brought Lilly into a hug.

"Lilly." He turned her to face him. "You are at Cirque to become a better you. Do it *for* your family. Let determination overcome your sadness."

"Okay." She wiped her tears, thinking about what Alfie had said. She followed him to the high beam.

She took a deep breath and held her head up. Before she knew it she had walked across the six-foot high beam without any assistance from her instructor. Her face lit up with excitement, "Alfie! Alfie! Did you see that?! I did it by myself!"

He laughed a hearty laugh, "Fantastic!" He clapped. "Now we move on." Lilly gulped. "Relax child, you'll do fine."

"Guys." Michael stood in front of the fireplace facing Lilly, Drew, Zoe and Jordan who all had their heads down and eyes closed.

"Go away," Zoe mumbled.

"Come on, let's go explore more of the circus. There's like a million doors to go through," Michael said with a slight whine to his voice.

No one paid him any mind. They continued to try to drift off to sleep.

"Seriously?" he exclaimed. "How can you possibly sleep right now? We're alive when we're all supposed to be dead, in a giant circus tent in some kind of freaky dimension and none of you want to go see what else is here?"

At that, all eyes opened.

"He has a point." Drew yawned and stood up beside Michael.

"Fine." Zoe lifted herself off of the couch.

"You coming Jordan?" Lilly asked him. His response was a slight nod and his movement off of the cozy armchair he had been reclined in.

Drew started to move towards the staircase leading to the Hall of Choice but he saw Michael moving to the right. "Where are you going?"

"There's a door at the end of this hallway."

He continued to walk down the dark purple hallway. Glittery gold swirls wound along the walls leading up to a door of the same color. "I wonder what's through here." Michael pulled open the door and stuck his head in.

"I don't think we're allowed to go through there," Lilly whispered. She shifted on her feet waiting for someone to yell at them for being somewhere they're not supposed to be.

"R.L. said we can go wherever we want." Michael opened the door completely and the group was greeted by a chorus of guitars, harmonicas, and loud voices.

Intrigued, they all stepped through the threshold.

CHAPTER 18. SIDE SHOW

S pread out before them was a neighborhood of multicolored tents. Strings of lights crisscrossed above them. Tall trees with twinkling lights lined a large path leading to a crowd of people singing, dancing, and laughing. Each teenager stood with wide eyes as they took in everything around them. A father walked past the group along with his wife and two children. They all had beards so long they touched the floor.

"What the—" Jordan was too shocked to form a complete sentence.

"Where are we?" Drew asked. He tilted his head and looked into the dazzling starry sky above him. He had never seen a night sky so clear. It was as if he could reach up and grab a handful of stars if he wanted to.

"Well, you're in the Side Show of course!" a voice from behind exclaimed. They turned to see a slim woman with big curly dark hair wearing a bright red leather jacket. "The home of fantastical creatures and ridiculous people! I'm Gina. You're the new recruits right?" the group nodded. "Well come on then! I'll show you around!" She walked through the middle of them and headed towards the wonderful commotion they heard.

The path they walked on was paved with dark blue stones, specks of something shiny in all of them, like stars nestled right under their feet.

"You see those right?" Lilly whispered to Zoe. She nodded her head as she continued to stare at the two gun holsters that were strapped to Gina's thighs.

"This is where all the Side Show acts live, the show before the actual show. Before and after Cirque performs people flock to see us," Gina boasted. "We have all sorts of wonders here! Tiny people that can fit right in the palm of your hand. Giant people who rattle the ground when they walk! Children with four eyes, adults with gills—all sorts of amazingly incredible things!" Gina's words came to life as she impersonated the people she described and spun around in a circle bursting with childlike excitement.

Most of them wouldn't admit it, but Gina's passion was contagious and every teenager felt their spirits lift and a sense of anticipation grow inside of them.

"What do you do in the Side Show?" Michael asked her.

Without any hesitation, Gina pulled out a pistol from the holster on her right leg. She looked to her right and the group followed suit. Through the trees, quite a distance off were two white balloons a few inches apart with what looked like a thin blade in between them. In an instant, Gina had aimed, breathed and shot. Her one bullet hit the blade, split into two, and both of the balloons popped at the same time.

"Woah," Jordan said.

Gina giggled, spun the gun around on her pointer finger, and strapped it back into the holster. Lilly watched as two more balloons inflated to replace the ones from before. *How?*

"There's lots of tricks to do with a pistol. Splitting a playing card in half, shooting backward while looking through a mirror—"

"Oh my gosh." Zoe almost tripped over her own feet when a little boy with four legs waved and smiled at her. She lifted her hand and smiled back hesitantly.

"That's Timmy," Gina told her as she waved at the boy and asked him how his mother was doing.

The further they walked into the Side Show, the more unbelievable it became. A couple with every inch of skin covered in tattoos and piercings, danced together happily swinging each other around to the rhythm of the music. The moonlight reflected off of the metal that covered their bodies. A woman with a face covered in hair, belted out a beautiful tune as she stood with the band. Two people were each playing a fiddle and were both completely white as snow, hair and skin and all. Next to them, a man played the guitar. He stood on legs that were backward, his feet facing behind him. Next to him, propped up on a red-painted wooden crate, was a woman with no lower body playing the accordion.

Zoe looked over a bit further and saw a man who sat amongst a group of children, amusing them with his ability to stretch out the skin on his face as if it were putty. Lilly didn't know whether to be impressed or frightened. A big part of her felt bad for all these people.

"Do not pity us, my dear." An elderly man wearing a long blue robe stopped the group in their tracks. His gray, almost translucent eyes, peered at Lilly.

"I don't mean to be rude," Lilly insisted. She tugged at the sleeves of her shirt like she always did when she was nervous.

"I know, it's okay. All of us here are quite unusual. We are freaks and we are okay with that. We are very proud of what we look like, as preposterous as it may seem to many." He smiled a genuine smile.

"This is Akili," Gina introduced. "He's very wise. He can read minds."

"Don't fear, I shall not intrude on private thoughts." He chuckled as the teenagers all relaxed. "We are marvelous creatures. Strange, yes, but marvelous and special all the same. There's a bit of bizarre in all of us, even in each of you. A strangeness that we tend to hide, but there is no reason to do such a thing," Akili spoke slowly, letting each word sink into the minds before him. "We are *all* freaks. It is okay to be different, to be peculiar, weird. I find it an incredible honor to be trusted with such remarkable gifts. It is a privilege to stand far apart from the crowd," Akili's voice was like a lullaby.

Lilly found herself nodding in agreement with him. She should be proud of who she was. A drumroll caught everyone's attention and Drew noticed the tower of smoke that was coming from up ahead.

"Oh!" Gina looked excitedly at the group and began to take off towards wherever the smoke was coming from. Akili said goodbye and the teenagers followed behind an eager Gina. Everyone seemed to be flocking to the same place. Children eagerly pushed through everyone else, all giggling and oozing happiness.

"What's happening?" Drew asked Gina over the noise of the crowd.

"Clyde of course!" she hollered over her shoulder.

"Of course," Jordan mumbled.

They stopped right behind Gina and she pulled all of them to sit on a bench in front of her. A warm fire burned in the middle of the crowd and all eyes were focused on a ridiculously large man. He laughed at something someone was saying and when he did every person could feel the deep booming in their stomachs. He smiled as everyone gathered close, looking at them and nodding a welcoming. The music around them softened as the crowd settled in.

"Clyde?" Michael asked Gina while motioning to the huge man. Gina nodded her head.

"Good evening, family!" Clyde shouted. The teens were taken aback at the loud whoops and hollers that came from all around them.

For a few minutes, the music quickened its pace again and the people of the Side Show broke out in boisterous conversation. Clyde lifted his hand and the volume lowered.

"You all look marvelous tonight," he had a booming voice, one that seemed to shake the ground with each word he spoke.

"You too, Clyde!" a few people shouted back at him. He laughed heartily.

Jordan guessed that he had to be about nine feet tall and at least five hundred pounds. He wore a white long sleeve shirt with a dark green vest. He had a bald head and bright green eyes.

"Clyde! Clyde!" a little girl yelled. She floated a few inches off the ground and was waving her hands in the air frantically.

"Yes, little one?" Clyde leaned towards her.

"Tell us a story!" the Side Show agreed loudly with her request.

"Any one in particular?" he asked her.

"The one about the hero and the evil and the battle! Please, Clyde!" a little boy with a lisp and one arm said.

Clyde laughed deeply, "Of course, little ones." He cleared his throat and waved his right hand in a circular motion three times. In response, the fire in front of them burned a light orange. "Since the beginning of time, there has been an Evil lurking in every corner. This Evil has been called several different names throughout history, but the motive has always stayed the same—to steal, to kill and to destroy anything and everything that is good." His accent was hard to decipher, mid-sentence it seemed to change. British to American to Indian to Spanish and so on. As if he spoke with every dialect there was.

"The Evil preys on fear and anxiety. It has a way of getting into minds and hearts, twisting good things into things of evil. All of humanity was hopeless and falling into the hands of the Evil constantly. It seemed as if there was no way out at all. A deep, dark sorrow fell over the world, causing even the land to decay. Humanity's insides were crying out, but the skin that they wore rarely showed the despair they locked away.

"All the while, in the midst of suffering, most of humanity did not know that a hero had been born. He was making his way into his destiny, a destiny that would change everything. The hero was a miracle birth and a strange child who turned into an even stranger man. In a world of sadness and cruelty, he was kind and gentle. He welcomed everyone, rich and poor, big and small, good and bad, to sit and be with him. He had miraculous magic flowing inside of him. He could heal hearts and bodies. He could bend the oceans to his will. No one had ever seen this kind of power before. He was a novelty. He was a freak—"

"Like us!" a child shouted. The crowd laughed.

"Yes child, just like us. The freak of all freaks! The King of the StrangeOnes," the crowd cheered and stomped. "A lot of the world didn't like that he was so different. He was the talk of every town. People spoke good and bad things about him. The man had a great purpose, and he knew it, and he knew that it was one that would cause him pain, but for the sake of helping others, he pursued it. He was the one who would battle the Evil. *He* was the hope for all."

Clyde waved his hand in three circles again and the fire changed to a deep red. Every person under the sound of his voice was captivated by the tale he was weaving. He looked over at the group of teenagers. They had all subconsciously leaned forward, eager to hear the rest of the story.

Clyde continued, "The hero went from city-to-city, town-to-town, wanting to meet as many people as he possibly could. He wanted to touch and speak to the people who needed his help. The Evil was tearing and destroying whatever it could get its hands on. In places where it left its cold dark touch, the hero would come with light and undo what the Evil had done. Some people welcomed him, some did not. Not everyone wanted what the hero had to give. Some thought he was crazy, that he was a fraud. There were people who the Evil had tricked and messed up their minds. They were making a plan to get rid of the hero.

"They wanted to kill him, to prove to everyone that he was a fake, that nothing he said or did was true. One day the hero stood and looked the Evil right in the face. The people gathered to watch their hero take down their enemy once and for all, but that was not what was to happen that day. Instead, the hero stood submissive and allowed the Evil to take him away. Down, down, down into the dark depths of our world he went. The people were devastated. "'There goes our one chance!' they cried."

As Clyde spoke the dialogue of the story, his voice transformed to sound like a crowd of a hundred people. Everyone around the fire felt as though they were living every moment of the story. "'Now what are we to do?' they exclaimed. They were angry and hurt and broken-hearted over the loss of a man they had all come to call friend. But their eyes could not see everything that was happening below the surface. The hero allowed himself to be taken by the Evil yes, but no matter what, whenever you bring light into darkness the darkness will be no more.

"The hero battled the Evil and he locked it up and made sure that every single person knew it." Clyde looked around at the smiling children. "But, there is always more to the hero than anyone could ever know. Evil is locked away yes, but it still finds its way out sometimes. That does not mean people have been abandoned by the hero though. If they need help all they must do is simply shout his name and he is there. Evil is not the absence of a hero, but giving in to the Evil is caused by the absence of being *close* to the hero. Many believe the hero still lives on today somewhere. Still helping, still smiling, and still sending the Evil back to where it belongs. The ancient text that tells the tale, says that one day the hero will truly defeat the Evil and everything will be at peace. Someday, an epic battle will be held and all of the world will see."

The flames exploded into white sparks lighting up the sky above the people and then fell softly down like snow. The fire in the middle turned low and dark orange. The crowd applauded and the children ran off to reenact the story. Clyde motioned the teenagers over to him. None of them moved until Gina pushed the entire bench forward with her feet, causing them all to stand.

"I'm Clyde. Welcome to Cirque, and welcome to the Side Show." Clyde stood.

"That was a great story," Zoe said. None of them knew quite what to say. They all craned their necks to look at Clyde.

"Thank you, my dear. I'm glad you enjoyed it." He looked at her arm and then said, "Contortionist, congratulations. So you've all been marked then?" They nodded. "A quiet group, eh?" he sat down and laughed causing the ground to slightly tremble. His laugh was so contagious that even a small smile came upon Jordan's face. "Which one of you have tried to leave the circus already?"

Everyone looked slightly to Jordan, except for Michael who pointed and said, "Him."

Clyde laughed again.

"How'd you know?" Jordan asked him.

"Somebody always tries to leave at some point. It can be a lot to take in."

"Do they always end up staying?" Jordan wondered.

Clyde frowned at this. "Unfortunately not. Sometimes they ignore R.L.'s pleas and walk through the door, never to return. It's always heartbreaking when it happens. A sadness like no other overcomes our precious Ringleader."

Jordan was quiet at that. He still felt a little guilty about trying to leave. But why should he? It didn't matter what these people thought or felt. He told R.L. he'd give this place one chance. *One chance,* he echoed in his mind.

"Are you allowed to tell us where we are? And I swear if you say 'you're with R.L.' I'm going to scream." Michael stepped close to Clyde.

The giant man bellowed out laughs causing everyone to giggle. They loved to hear him laugh.

"You're in a magical place," Clyde's voice lowered. The fire turned purple as he spoke. "A place that could change everything for you. A place that has been waiting, a place that was made," Clyde paused for a second, "for *you.*" He made eye contact with each one of the teenagers. The group waited for more but it was clear that was all Clyde was going to give them.

"Thanks for clearing that up," Zoe told him sarcastically.

Lilly let out a yawn and covered her mouth embarrassed.

Clyde laughed. "It is quite late, you should probably be heading back. I wish you all the best of luck in your endeavors. You are always welcome here. You are family now."

"Thanks." Michael shook his hand.

"I'll walk you out," Gina offered. They passed through the Side Show performers once again. Everyone wished the group a good night. "Don't be strangers okay? Come visit again." Gina told them.

"We will." Drew smiled. Gina held the door open for everyone and waved one last time before closing it.

"Dang, how long were we in there?" Zoe asked. The Commons was empty, though the fireplaces still burned.

"I didn't even realize how tired I was." Drew rubbed his eyes. They slowly walked to their rooms and saw Barnaby waiting in the hallway.

"Welcome back." He closed his pocket watch and smiled.

"We didn't mean to be gone so long," Lilly apologized.

"It's no problem, no problem at all. I just wanted to make sure you didn't get lost. Cirque can be very confusing."

"Foreal." Jordan went to his door.

"I'll see you all bright and early at breakfast. Sweet dreams." Barnaby hurried off and the group diverged.

"That was a great story, huh?" Drew asked as he got settled into the bottom bunk.

"It was alright," Jordan spoke flatly.

"Why just alright?" Drew had been enthralled with the prospect of such an amazing hero.

"It's just so fake. There's no way anyone like that could ever exist. There's not some Evil trying to get into our heads and ruin our lives. And there's no hero trying to beat it. There's just the world as we know it." Jordan paused. Then, quieter, he said, "Besides, if there were a hero, he would've helped me out a long time ago."

An awkward sadness interrupted the conversation. That was the most Jordan had ever spoken, the first time he had expressed how he felt or thought. Jordan looked quickly to try and see

Drew and Michael's expressions. He didn't mean to bring the room down. *I'm just speaking truth,* he told himself. *They can believe in that stuff if they want, but I won't. There's no way. Life is just life, just the way it is. Nothing more to it.*

After a long silence Michael, in a nonchalant tone of voice said, "I figure anything's possible at this point." He yawned and stretched out on his bed. "I mean, we just sat around a color-changing campfire next to a mermaid in a fish tank, and now we're sleeping in a circus to wake up and train in life-endangering acts." He laughed lightly at his own statement.

"It's too good to be true," Jordan mumbled as he rolled over in bed.

Michael and Drew laid in their beds going back and forth in their minds. A part of them wanted to believe wholeheartedly in a hero, but the other part knew that Jordan was right. If a hero did exist, life would have been very different.

CHAPTER 19. PAIN IS PAIN

R.L. sat in the Commons the next morning with a red leather-bound journal in his hand. The covers of it had carvings in all kinds of languages. Names filled all the pages, scribbled in different sizes and inks. Some crammed into the margins, some even written upside down. There were hundreds of pages in the journal, every single one covered in writing.

Zoe looked over R.L.'s shoulder. She leaned on the back of the armchair he was sitting in. The fire crackled in the Commons while people came and went from the dining hall for breakfast. Zoe had been up before the rest of the group, the nightmares still managing to make an appearance. They were less gruesome each time, but her mind wouldn't let her sleep.

She asked him, "What is that?"

R.L. whispered, "Hurting people." He ran his fingers along the pages.

"That's a lot of names," her voice was quiet.

R.L. gently closed the journal. He looked at it with sorrowful, thoughtful eyes. "Everyone hurts Zoe. No one is an exception to that. No matter what they or anyone else may think."

She nodded slightly.

"Still having bad dreams?" he asked her.

"How did you know?" Before R.L. replied Zoe said, "Right, you know everything." R.L. smiled and nodded. She sighed and then told him, "Yeah, every night. They're not as bad as when they first started, but—" she trailed off.

"Even when we are away from the things that caused us pain, they still manage to hurt us. It's all in the mind. It's learning to think differently, which comes from healing. And you will heal Zoe."

"How?"

"Continue what you're doing. Training, making friends, learning from those around you, and learning about yourself."

Before Zoe could reply, Drew ran into the Commons, "R.L.! R.L.!" The Ringleader jumped up out of the chair. "It's Jordan and Michael!" R.L. and Zoe followed Drew quickly to the hallway outside the bedrooms.

Lilly stared at herself in the mirror. She stood in the bathroom that was connected to the bedroom. She didn't bother wiping the tears from her eyes. She hadn't looked at herself once since coming to Cirque, and now that she had, she instantly regretted it. She was reminded of every imperfection on her face and body. The food she had been eating was catching up to her. She didn't have makeup on, her hair wasn't done, even the clothes she was wearing made her look like a slob. She hiccuped as she cried and eyed the toilet.

"You don't know a damn thing about me!" Lilly was caught off guard by Michael's yelling coming from the hallway.

"There's nothin' to know! You got everything you ever wanted while others barely got by!" Jordan yelled back. He clenched his jaw and ground his teeth together.

Lilly opened her bedroom door quietly to see what was happening.

"My family had money because my father wasn't a drunk loser like yours probably was." Michael took a step forward and poked Jordan tauntingly in the chest. "If I were you, I'd take pointers from me so you don't end up just like him!"

Jordan pushed Michael with all his might and drew his fist back.

"Hey!" R.L. appeared and jumped in the middle of them. Drew and Zoe stood by the stairs. "Enough," the Ringleader said. Jordan didn't relax his hand. "Come with me." R.L began to turn down the hallway. Neither of the boys moved. They were locked in a tension-filled stare. "Now." R.L. left no room for argument, they reluctantly followed.

"Well that was intense," Drew said once they were gone.

"What happened?" Zoe asked.

"I don't know, I heard them yelling from our room," said Lilly. "I wonder where R.L.'s taking them."

"Well, wherever it is I definitely don't want to be there. Do you think he's gonna kick them out?" Zoe asked. Drew and Lilly shrugged. Zoe asked them, "You wanna go back to the Side Show? We have some time before training."

"I might catch up to you," Drew said walking downstairs.

"Did you eat breakfast?" Zoe asked Lilly as they walked to the Side Show.

"I wasn't hungry."

"Are you sure?" Lilly just nodded and smiled, just like she used to do at home to her mother. Her stomach turned in uneasiness and hunger, but she wasn't about to let anyone know.

"If you ever want to talk, I'll listen," Zoe told her.

"Thanks." Lilly considered taking her up on that offer.

Drew wandered around aimlessly before winding up in the Hall of Choice. He debated which door he should go through if he should go through any at all. One full turn later, Drew grasped the knob of the Door of Desire.

"Where are we going?" Michael asked.

R.L. had led them through several hallways in complete silence. Michael's question went unanswered as they continued walking. Finally, R.L. stopped in front of a door and stood aside. He nodded for the boys to go through it.

Jordan and Michael stood in the middle of an empty room. The walls were gray and without windows.

"Alright, hit me," R.L. said.

"What?" they asked in unison.

"Hit me. You were about to hit each other and I'm not going to let that happen so hit me instead." They just looked at him. "C'mon!"

"I'm not gonna hit you, man," Jordan said.

"Why not?"

"My problem's not with you," Jordan told him.

"Jordan, have you not learned by now that violence affects everyone surrounding it? Whether you hit each other or you hit me, I get hurt. As do the two of you and everyone in Cirque. We are a family, and family here does not hurt each other. Ever." Jordan looked away. Michael drummed his fingers against his thigh anxiously. "Now, what was the problem?" R.L. asked them.

"He tried to act like he knew me. Saying that he understood what my life was like. He had no right," Jordan said. He waved his arms emphatically, his voice rising with anger.

"Why not?" R.L. challenged.

"He's got no clue how I grew up!"

"If people are at the bottom, it's their own fault," Michael said.

"My mother does not deserve to live how she has to live!" Jordan got right in

Michael's face.

"She should leave your father then if it's that bad!"

"You don't know what it's like, stop acting like you got all the answers!"

"Enough!" R.L. stopped their arguing. The boys backed away from each other, each breathing heavily. "It is not right for either of you to judge. You come from different families, different lifestyles but you have much more in common than you think."

Michael laughed. "Like what?"

R.L. looked each boy in the eye and then reached out both arms to touch their foreheads with his pointer and middle finger.

Jordan opened his eyes to see he was sitting at the dinner table. There was a boy sitting across from him, a woman at the end of the table and a man at the other end. They were all talking, it was muffled at first but then began to clear up.

"Michael?" the man said. "Michael, boy, I'm talking to you." Jordan looked at the man confused. The man slammed his hand on the table causing the dinnerware to shake. "Boy, don't make me come over there." Jordan nodded his head slowly. *What is going on? This must be R.L.'s doing.*

"Michael, your report card came in the mail," the woman spoke.

"Unacceptable," the man said. "More C's than A's, notes on behavior problems—what's the matter with you? I didn't raise a stupid son!" Again he slammed his hand on the table and Jordan flinched. The boy sitting across from him just smiled.

"Your brother got perfect A's and is on the honor roll. You have no excuse," the woman said.

Jordan felt like crying. He couldn't understand why. This must've been what Michael felt. He looked down at his hands, they looked small. He looked up and saw his reflection in the glass of a china cabinet. A boy that couldn't have been more than twelve was staring back—Michael. He was living this moment as Michael.

"Go to your room. No dinner tonight. You're grounded for a month. You will do your homework every day in this room and extra work on top of that. Do you understand?" Jordan just looked at the man as he spoke angrily. A vein was popping out of his forehead and his fists were clenched. He looked so mean, so cold. Then the man stood up and within a second he had smacked Jordan on the back of the head. "ROOM NOW!"

Jordan ran through the house not knowing where to go, just having an overwhelming feeling of wanting to run away. He wanted to go somewhere his family could never find him.

Jordan opened his eyes to see R.L. and Michael. He looked down at his hands and his clothes, he was himself again. Michael was conscious, too, his eyes glassy with unshed tears. Jordan knew his eyes looked the same.

"What was that?" Jordan didn't expect his voice to break.

Michael opened his mouth to say something but was at a loss for words. He couldn't remember the last time he had been speechless.

R.L. said, "You both come from homes where family was a monster itself. You were neglected, alone, and terrified of the future. Neither of you knows who you are and you're both struggling not to be like your fathers. You both feel lost."

"How did you do—" Michael was cut off as R.L. continued.

"Just because someone's situation might not seem as bad as yours, it is just as bad to them. Everyone's pain matters and everyone feels pain. There's no need to compare, no need to fight. Michael, there is always a reason why someone is living the way they are. Part of it is a personal choice and part of it is out of their control. You have no right to judge someone based on circumstances. You have no idea what chain of events occurred in their life." Michael hung his head in shame.

"Jordan, if you would stop pushing people away you wouldn't feel so alone. You wouldn't always have to be ready to fight and defend yourself. You would have good people standing with you, to fight *for* you. You both would understand each other a lot more if you looked past money, lifestyle, appearance—all the things that don't even matter."

They were silent for a few moments, lost in thought.

"Now what?" Jordan asked.

"I'm asking for both of you to let your guard down and try to understand each other. I'm asking you to look at each other as equals. When you were home you might have been complete opposites, but now you're in Cirque," R.L. paused. "And in Cirque we are family. Family doesn't always get along, but they are always there for each other. Neither of you knows what that's like, but you will learn it here. You were brothers the moment you opened your eyes in my circus tent."

Jordan and Michael looked at each other, and for the first time, actually considered seeing each other.

After a moment Michael stuck his hand out, "Brothers."

Jordan's first instinct was to slap his hand away, but instead he looked at R.L. Then, he looked back at Michael and remembered the scared little boy he saw in the reflection. "Brothers," he agreed. They shook hands.

The Door of Desire opened to a peaceful small-town neighborhood. The grass was so green Drew had to feel it to see whether or not it was real. The sun was bright, but not so much that it blinded him; it was just right. Drew stood in the middle of a perfectly paved street. The sky was a beautiful blue. The air smelled of Spring and barbecue.

He looked behind him, but the door he had come through was nowhere in sight. A conversation coming from behind one of the houses brought Drew out of his thoughts. His curiosity led him to a backyard filled with people. They all looked perfect. No hair out of place, no wrinkle in their clothes, and perfect pearly white smiles. Children jumped on a trampoline and adults laughed sophisticatedly with a glass of wine in hand.

"Drew!" Drew's head snapped up to a familiar face.

"Mom?" he choked the word out. He almost cried at the sight of her.

"I saved you some food. Come." She smiled warmly and grabbed his hand. Drew followed in utter bewilderment. Anna shoved a heavy plate of food in his hands. It smelled incredible, his mouth watered.

"There's my boy!" Frank clapped Drew on the back and led him over to a group of colleagues. Drew looked to his mom for an explanation but she was paying no mind. Drew's body began to slightly shake. He was so nervous, his dad was never like this with him. "This is my son, Drew." he introduced him. The men said their hellos. "I tell you, this boy's got brains like no other. I have no clue where they came from though." They all laughed. "We're so proud of him," his father said.

Drew stood there, thankful that his father had his arm around him otherwise he would have fallen over from shock. Frank continued to talk about how proud he was to have Drew as a son. Drew searched for sarcasm, but there was not a trace in Frank's tone. He was being sincere.

Something was terribly wrong.

"Um," Drew cleared his throat. "I'll, I'll be right back." He set his plate of food down and ran into the house before anyone could see the tears in his eyes.

He went into the bathroom and splashed cold water on his face. He bent over the sink and shut his eyes tightly. His whole life he had waited to hear his father say those words. *"I'm proud."* And now, they tumbled out of his mouth so effortlessly. Drew took deep breaths, in and out, in and out. He wiped his eyes. *What is going on?* Drew thought to himself. *Am I back home? Is this after they found my body? Am I alive? Did we all make amends? Was Cirque just a dream?*

After taking a deep breath, Drew opened his eyes and jumped back in shock. The mirror that hung above the sink suffered from cracks that hadn't been there a minute before. The sink was filled with black slime. He looked up at the now dimming light. Drew opened the bathroom door. The entire house was destroyed. Cobwebs lurked in every corner, dust coated every surface. Table legs were broken, chairs knocked over, and there was a gaping hole in the living room wall.

Drew walked to the suddenly empty backyard. The sky was overcast and the air was cold. There was a stench unlike anything Drew had smelled before. The grass was dead and overtaken by weeds. Every house he could see looked like it had been through a natural disaster. In only a matter of minutes, this whole world had become the complete opposite of what it had been when Drew first arrived.

He walked into the street calling for his parents. An eerie quiet was the only response. He wanted to see them again, to hear his dad say those words again. *"I'm proud."* The street and sidewalk were just as ruined as the houses. Large cracks and holes covered the pavement.

Drew heard what sounded like dragging feet. He turned around and his eyes combed over the neighborhood residents.

They were covered in dirt and were walking slowly, seeming oblivious to everything.

"Mom?" Anna's body straightened up and her red eyes met her son's worried ones.

Within a second she had started sprinting towards Drew. The neighborhood followed right behind her. Drew could tell by the way his mom narrowed her eyebrows and screamed that she wasn't running to him for a warm embrace. Adrenaline kicked in and Drew sped off looking for somewhere to hide. His eyes searched for the gold door but it wasn't anywhere. Panic pushed him to run faster. His labored breathing hurt his chest, but his feet paid no mind.

He veered left, hoping to find refuge in one of the wrecked houses. From behind the house came another group of neighbors. Drew stopped short and ran to another backyard. Stretched before him, all he could see were endless dead fields and dark skies. He turned around and felt like he was the lone survivor in a zombie movie. He shivered as he imagined his flesh being chewed on by his own parents.

Suddenly, a bright light came from the ground and blinded Drew's attackers.

"R.L.!" Drew screamed in relief.

"Quick, through the door!" R.L. told him.

"Where?"

"Behind you!" Drew turned, swung the door open and jumped through. He landed face-first in the hallway. R.L. walked gracefully through the door a moment later.

Drew took deep breaths to slow his heart down. "What was that place? I thought that door was supposed to take me to what I want."

R.L. reached out a hand and helped Drew stand. "Most of the time what we desire is not what we need."

"Everything was so perfect though. Well, perfect until—"

"Until the true nature was shown," R.L. told him.

"I don't understand. My dad he, he said—" Drew stopped himself. He squeezed his eyes shut, trying not to cry.

R.L. pulled Drew into a hug. Drew was stiff at first, he couldn't remember the last time he had been hugged. He let himself sink into R.L. though and he wrapped his arms around him. He felt relief rush through him. They pulled away but R.L. kept his hand on Drew's shoulder.

"We all think we know what's best. We think we know what will make life good, what will make us feel better. Money, clothes, promotions. We believe that if we just have this one thing then everything will be perfect. For you, it is acceptance. If your father loves you for who you are then life will be easy."

"It won't?" Drew's chest tightened.

"Life will never be easy, but it will be easier when you learn to love yourself and surround yourself with people who love you the correct way. Your happiness cannot depend on others. If you let it, then you will never be free from the pain that you've been holding on to. You may never have the relationship you want with your father. I do believe people can change, but you can't wait for him for you to be happy. You have to first learn to be happy with yourself."

Drew's eyebrows creased as he thought that over.

R.L. offered a smile, "Come on." He threw an arm around Drew's shoulders and they walked back towards the circus ring where Wyatt smiled warmly.

"You okay?" he asked Drew.

Drew nodded.

"Come on." They walked over to their training area and R.L. scanned the room.

Lilly was listening to Alfie's instructions, Zoe was laughing with Abrielle, and Michael and Jordan were taking a water break near the bleachers. R.L. laughed when he noticed Dez and Annette waiting impatiently.

"What did you see?" Jordan asked. Michael sipped his water.

"Your house. You, or I, walked into the living room and your parents were getting high. Your mom told you to go to your room but I felt like I had to help her. Your dad didn't like that and he hit me, or you, and pushed me back into your room."

Jordan nodded remembering that night. "I eventually crawled down the fire escape and went and got high myself. Figured if they were gonna do it there was nothin' stopping me," Drew told him.

"I'm sorry," Michael sighed.

"Me too," Jordan said.

CHAPTER 20. DOUBT

"I'm not a huge fan of surprises," Lilly told Alfie.

She stood with her eyes closed. Another day of training filled the circus ring with excitement, encouraging voices and music.

"This is so exciting!" Mia and Milo said in shrill voices.

"Ready, Lilly?" Alfie asked.

"I don't know," Lilly said, cringing.

"Open your eyes." She did so slowly. Her mouth opened in surprise when she saw what Alfie was holding out for her.

"Those are mine?" She took the slippers from his hands and felt the leather material.

"You are ready to walk the ropes."

"They're so beautiful." They were a light brown color and had a pink cursive L sewn into the sides.

"Well, put them on, Lilly!" Mia said clapping her hands.

Lilly sat down and slid her feet into the slippers. "So stretchy."

"Yes. It is like being barefoot. The leather allows for flexibility while protecting your feet from injury," Alfie told her.

"So cool." She stood up and walked around a bit.

"Now that you are familiar with them. We move to the rope." Alfie smiled.

"What?" She followed Alfie to where the other Tightrope Walkers were practicing.

"Don't you think it's too early for me to be doing this?" Lilly asked. She stepped on top of a small platform three feet off the ground with a rope outstretched before her leading to another platform.

"You can do this. Just move slowly and listen to my instructions."

Lilly took a deep breath.

"Stretch your arms out, put your shoulders back, and your head up." Alfie inspected her posture, he tilted her chin up a little more. "Good. Now, here." He placed a book on top of her head.

"What are you doing?" She looked at him and the book slipped off. He caught it effortlessly.

"Without having a strong center of mass you will never correctly walk across any rope. This book will help you keep your posture. Your center must be directly over the rope. Now breathe."

And she did.

"Ahhh!" Lilly screamed as she fell off the rope. Alfie swiftly caught her.

"It's okay. Try again." He placed her back on the platform.

"But I fell," Lilly said close to tears.

"And now you're standing," Alfie smiled. "The most important choice you can make is what you do after you fall. Will you stay down? Or will you stand?"

Lilly nodded and put her shoulders back. She put the book on top of her head, looked at the rope in front of her, and put one foot in front of the other.

"It's getting easier isn't it?" Abrielle asked Zoe as she stretched into simple yoga positions.

"Yeah, actually," Zoe admitted.

"The more you stretch and practice, the more comfortable you'll become. Soon it'll be second nature." Abrielle smiled big as she watched Zoe ease into a split.

"How long have you been a Contortionist?" Zoe asked her instructor.

"Long time."

"Did R.L. bring you here after you died, too?" The girls sat across from each other, Zoe eagerly waiting for a response and Abrielle trying to orchestrate one.

"Sort of. I met R.L. a long time ago. He found me when I was hurting. I didn't exactly die though."

"Who hurt you?" Zoe pressed.

"I had bad taste in men. I was with someone who hurt me real bad."

Zoe nodded. "I get that."

"Yeah?"

"My dad left, my stepfather hurt me."

Abrielle didn't say anything, but she didn't need to. Just looking in each other's eyes spoke volumes. Zoe felt as though someone understood her, that she wasn't alone in her pain. She had never felt that way before, strengthened by someone else.

"Being a Contortionist saved my life," Abrielle told her.

"How?"

"Gave me a reason to fight. You'll see for yourself, too."

Clank! Clank! Clank! The swords clanged together as Wyatt and Drew danced around each other.

"Good!" Wyatt told Drew as he stepped around.

"Ah!" Drew exclaimed. Wyatt spun his sword around and around Drew's sword until Drew's wrist twisted and his sword fell to the ground. "Couldn't have let me have that one?" Drew asked. He rubbed his wrist.

"Gotta' learn." Wyatt laughed.

"Let's go again then!" Drew picked up his sword and stood on guard.

Annette instructed Jordan, "Okay, now spin the torch."

Jordan attempted to spin the torch without setting his shirt on fire, but it was no use. He patted the flames away and threw the torch on the ground with an aggravated yell.

"It's okay. Try again," Annette's voice was calm and sooth-ing, which just made Jordan angrier.

"That was my seventh time trying! I can't do this!" Jordan yelled. The other Fire Breathers stopped to watch the commo-tion.

"Yes, you can!" Annette yelled back, startling him. "You see that mark on your arm?" She grabbed his arm and pointed. "See that tattoo?" Jordan looked down at the mark. "You were meant for this."

"I keep getting burned," he said calmer now.

She let go of him and waved her arms around dramatically. "Of course, you're getting burned. It's fire!" She flicked his ear.

"Ow," he let a laugh slip through.

She grabbed his ear and gently pulled him down a few inch-es so they were face to face. "Learn to overcome it. Stop believ-ing that it has more power than you do. Bend the fire to *your* will."

Jordan rubbed his ear when she let go and sent her a glare. She just smiled at him. He picked up his torch again and spun it slowly. Eventually, his spin got faster. He was actually doing it. Maybe she was right. Maybe R.L. was right. He excitedly looked up at Annette and then lost concentration. He yelled as he rubbed the fresh burn on his arm.

"Told ya' you could do it," Annette said as she bandaged him up.

"Where is Michael?" Dez asked the other Trapeze Artists. They all shrugged their shoulders. "He is going to drive me to insanity." He continued to stomp around, looking for his wandering trainee.

Michael walked around exploring the circus, feeling no obligation whatsoever to go to training. There were so many doors and so many pictures on the walls. He wanted to see everything; he wanted to figure this place out.

"Michael." He jumped and let out a yelp at R.L.'s sudden appearance in front of him. When the smoke cleared he saw the Ringleader looking at him with a raised eyebrow.

"Woah." It was the first time R.L. wasn't wearing his purple coat and Michael was mesmerized by R.L.'s arms.

They were both covered in amazing tattoos. His left arm was completely dark blue down to his wrist. Planets and moons were spinning and twinkling stars were scattered among beautifully colored galaxies, pink and gray and purple. Michael felt like he was looking through a telescope. On R.L.'s right arm from the elbow down to his wrist was the sea. Inside of the light blue waters were all different kinds of fish and sea creatures swimming around. From his elbow up, it looked like a rainforest. Beautiful green trees stood tall with birds flying around and jungle creatures perched on the branches.

"Michael," R.L.'s voice was stern.

"Nice tattoos, how do they move?"

"Michael." He looked up to R.L.'s face.

"Why are you not in training?"

Michael shrugged his shoulders, "Not really feeling it."

"Why is that?"

"I don't want to train." Michael looked at one of the portraits on the wall. "Can you believe people actually used to dress like that?" He chuckled but R.L. stayed serious.

"Michael, what's the real reason you're not in training?"

Michael sighed and looked at the ground. It took him a minute to decide to tell the truth. "I can't do it," he spoke quietly.

"Can't do what?"

"I can't be a Trapeze Artist!" he was a little louder this time, annoyed at his own insecurities.

"What's stopping you?" R.L. asked softly.

"I just can't."

"That's not a real reason."

"I'm not good at it."

"You haven't even done it yet."

"Exactly! I'm just doing simple stuff and I can barely do that right. I'm not cut out for this. The others, they're doing great but I can't." Michael avoided eye contact with the Ringleader.

"Michael, that mark on your arm is there for a reason. You are the only one that can fulfill your purpose. You were meant for the trapeze. You will surprise yourself with how well you'll do. Don't let yourself stop you. Believe that you can do it and you will."

"Maybe I was marked with the wrong thing," Michael challenged.

"You weren't. The Marks are never wrong."

Michael shrugged.

"This is for you, no one else. You are not doing it for recognition or praise. You are doing it because you deserve a meaningful life. You deserve a purpose."

Michael nodded, looking into his eyes, trying to believe him.

"And you better hurry back to the ring because Dez is ripping up floorboards looking for you."

"Great." Michael sauntered off and R.L. sighed.

"They are ours." R.L. turned around when he heard the whisper. He walked down the hallway looking for open doors or windows. There was nothing.

"No," he spoke loudly so they could hear. "They. Are. Not."

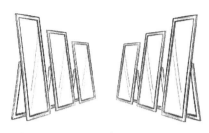

CHAPTER 21.
FREEDOM IS A CHOICE

Jordan stood alone in the Hall of Choice, staring at his reflection. The door beckoned him to come inside, but he couldn't do it. He was so scared to see his future. He had already made up his mind about what it was going to look like. He was going to see himself as his father. Angry, alone and empty inside. He was already halfway there.

Jordan clenched his fist out of his fear to see himself like that. He hated his father, but he was convinced he was going to become him. *Life is cruel like that*, Jordan thought to himself. *How did it even happen?* He wondered. He remembers clearly, constantly, promising to never become like either one of his parents.

At some point in time, he must've given up that dream. At some point in time, nature must've taken over and without him realizing it, he started to become like the one he hated most. And then, he began to hate himself. *The stupid, sick cycle.*

"I regret to inform you that you lack the telekinetic abilities necessary to open the door with just a look." R.L.'s reflection appeared beside Jordan's. "You'll have to physically turn the knob to go inside."

"Behind this door is what could be?" Jordan's quiet voice, barely audible, echoed in the Hall.

R.L. nodded. Jordan looked so vulnerable in front of the door.

Jordan continued to stare.

"Why don't you open it?" R.L. whispered.

"I'm scared," Jordan whispered back.

He closed his eyes tightly. He imagined his father's reaction to that statement. He would have smacked him on the back of the head. *"What kind of man are you? I didn't raise my son to be a coward."* His words would be filled with anger and disgust. He would've pushed Jordan around, taunting him, calling him every name in the book to degrade him. In his own head, Jordan would have said, *you didn't raise your son at all.*

"Ah, fear, the great preventer," R.L. said as he leaned against his cane with his right hand and took off his hat with his left.

Jordan was quiet, reliving his father's most brutal moments.

"It's okay to be scared, Jordan." The teenager smiled. Such a different reaction from what he was used to. "What are you scared of Jordan?" The Ringleader asked.

"I don't want to become my father."

"You don't have to."

"Do I really have any other options?" Jordan backed away from the door and gave his full attention to R.L. He couldn't bear to look at himself anymore.

"You have a world of opportunities waiting for you."

"Nah, there's nothing for me. I've got no skills, I was a terrible student, I've got no money. There's nowhere for me to go."

"Those are excuses, Jordan. If you really want something you can make it happen. There are thousands of successful people who started with absolutely nothing but pain."

"Well, I've got that covered, huh?" Jordan laughed dryly.

"With pain, you can either thrive or die. That choice is completely on you, no one can take the blame when it comes to that one. There comes a point where you have to stop being the victim." R.L. put his hat back on and stood up straight.

"Thrive or die," Jordan repeated, letting the words take on meaning in his life.

"You have a world of opportunities waiting for you," R.L. said it slower this time, grabbing Jordan's shoulder and making eye contact. R.L. needed him to get this.

"I might fail."

"You might succeed."

"I just..."

"Jordan." the Ringleader gave Jordan's shoulder a firm reassuring grip. "Freedom is yours, but so is the choice." Jordan looked at R.L., and then at the door.

"Will you go in with me?" Jordan asked.

R.L. nodded.

Jordan felt relieved, which freaked him out. Without even realizing it, he had come to depend on the Ringleader. That had not been part of the plan. Jordan never asked anyone for help, he had to do everything himself otherwise he was weak. *Right?* Memories filled his head. Never asking for help in school, from his friends, from Blight. *Guess all it took was dying to finally knock some sense into me.*

He briefly glanced at R.L. and tried to control his emotions. This stranger, this weird dude in fancy coats and top hats, cared. *He cares so much that he's put up with all my bs*, Jordan shook his head at the thought.

"Why do you care so much about me?" he had to force the words out of his mouth.

R.L. smiled. "You deserve to be cared about Jordan. You're important. You may think it's strange for me, someone who you feel barely knows you, to care. But, to me, it's simple, easy. You're a great person, with great things to bring to the world. You're a person who had a tough life, circumstances stacked against him. I would have to be crazy *not* to care." R.L.'s eyes filled with unshed tears.

Jordan chuckled.

"I know it can be hard to ask for help," R.L. said. "To have to trust someone with parts of your life, to have to lean on someone else sometimes. But no one is meant to do life alone." He squeezed Jordan's shoulder lovingly. "It's not in our nature. You will always go farther when you walk with others, they help you up when you fall. When you're alone, it gets harder to pick yourself up time after time. It's okay to let other people do it for you when you need it. I even have to surround myself with others. Barnaby is stronger than he looks, he has helped me up many times."

Jordan smiled at the mental image of four-foot something Barnaby picking up six-foot R.L.

"You can do this, Jordan."

"Okay." He took a deep breath and grasped the cold steel doorknob. He opened the Door of Opportunity.

He was speechless as he looked around the room. Everything was white. The floors, the ceiling, the walls, and the stands that held thousands of mirrors. The room seemed to span forever. Mirror, after mirror, after mirror.

"Go on." R.L. nudged him forward.

Jordan walked slowly to a mirror. His stomach was twisting up in nerves, his mind was swirling with thoughts. He almost couldn't breathe when he saw his reflection. The Jordan he saw was looking back at him was smiling and wearing a suit. He was standing in an office with a giant window overlooking a city. The little sign on the desk had CEO next to his name.

"No way," Jordan could hardly speak. His eyes blurred with tears.

He walked over to the next mirror. In this one, he was wearing a blue uniform standing in front of a police car. He laughed aloud at that one. He ran over to the next mirror, and then the next, and the next. He was standing in front of a classroom as a teacher, leading a group to help orphans in a foreign country, defending people in a courtroom, laughing with a wife and children around a dinner table in a happy home— he fully cried at that one.

He stood in front of one particular mirror for a long time. The Jordan looking back at him was wearing a lab coat and attending to sick children. He watched himself in awe, moving effortlessly through the hospital as people regarded him with respect, as families hugged him with tears of joy and words of thanks.

"My father told me I couldn't, I, I—"

"Who cares?" R.L. told Jordan. "Does your father write the future? How could he possibly know what you will or won't do? Everything he said to you was a lie. No one decides for you Jordan, no one but you."

Jordan couldn't tear his eyes away from the mirror. Tears streaming down his face he said, "Thrive or die."

"The choice is all on you. Life, or death. Freedom, or the way you're living life now."

Jordan nodded. He watched his doctor self for a little while longer. He needed to remember this image for the rest of his life.

"I'm going to the library if you guys wanna come," Zoe told Lilly and Drew who were in the middle of an intense checkers game.

"Just one more move and I'll annihilate her." Drew jumped over Lilly's remaining pieces and made it to the other side of the board to be kinged. Lilly laughed as Drew did a victory dance.

The three of them walked down the long hallway. It was brightly lit but strangely quiet. Lilly pretended to be listening as Drew told her about how he held an undefeated record in one of his online games. Zoe walked straight ahead lost in her thoughts. *Where was everybody?* Usually, the circus held non-stop noise. Suddenly, a figure came out of the dining room.

Zoe released a terrified scream. Lilly and Drew jumped in surprise.

"You almost made me drop the brownies!" Michael yelled at her.

"You scared me!" Zoe yelled back.

"Watch where you're going next time."

"What were you doing in there anyway? It's all dark," Zoe asked him.

"They put some desserts in plastic containers on the tables. I was hungry."

Zoe rolled her eyes at him.

"You know, someday your eyes are gonna get stuck like that," Michael told her.

"Did you guys see that?" Lilly asked after the lights flickered.

"Yeah," Michael said uneasily. The lights flickered again.

Drew rubbed his arms as goosebumps appeared. "It's not even cold," he said. "If anything, it's getting hotter."

"Something's wrong," Zoe said as the lights began to flash on and off.

Heavy footsteps brought an unusually tall muscular man to the group with a determined look on his mustached face. "To the Commons. You'll be safe." They obeyed his instructions without question. As they entered the Commons, R.L. and Jordan were coming down the stairs.

"General," R.L. greeted the man. "Light everything with a wick. Make sure all the doors are locked and that everyone remains in large groups," he spoke calmly.

"Copy." The General left in a hurry.

"What's happening?" Lilly asked.

With a snap of R.L.s fingers, hundreds of candles appeared in the room causing a glow to settle in. The fireplaces blazed making everyone even hotter. "Some unwelcome guests have arrived."

"Who?" Zoe asked. She rubbed her sweaty palms on her pants.

"We call them Shadow People," R.L. told them.

"I don't think I wanna know how they earned that name," Michael said. Lilly gulped. Drew nodded his head in agreement.

"Are they a threat?" Jordan asked.

"Only if you allow them to be. If you give in to the fear, anxiety, sadness or regret they bring. If they approach you do not look at them, no matter what. They show you what you fear most and it is not pretty what happens if you allow yourself to see."

"How did they get in?" Jordan tried to conceal his worry.

"That is an excellent question," R.L. said, angrily.

"R.L.! R.L.!" Wyatt ran into the room gasping for air. "The Shadows infiltrated all the habitats. The animals are freaking out, it's bad."

R.L. turned to the group, "I'll be back. The General has his crew patrolling everywhere. Stay together." He grabbed Wyatt's arm and they vanished immediately leaving behind the red glittery smoke.

"I feel like I'm in a horror movie," Zoe said as she sank deeper into the couch. "I hate horror movies."

"Scared you too bad?" Michael teased.

"I don't like when it's dead silent, and then the killer pops out and the stupid girl that walked into the basement alone lets out a scream and dies."

"R.L. said they can't hurt us unless we let them," Drew said aloud, mostly to comfort himself.

"What does that even mean?" Jordan asked.

A hissing sound entered the room.

Lilly's gut-wrenching scream made everyone's stomach drop.

Every candle blew out.

"Keep your eyes shut!" Jordan yelled.

Everything seemed so loud. A hot wind blew all around, tugging and pulling at the teens' clothes. Voices that sounded like nails on a chalkboard made everyone wince. Claws scratched at the floor. Doors opened and slammed shut over and over again. Glass shattered as if it were being thrown against every surface in the room.

"Zoe," she recognized Paul's voice. She screamed. His voice taunted her, "Zoe open your eyes."

"NO!" She hugged her knees closer. Her eyes were shut so tight it began to hurt.

"ZOE!" Paul's voice roared. It shook her to the core.

Her eyes shot open.

All she saw was black.

All she felt was fear.

A human-shaped figure stood before her. The figure twisted into a cloud of thick black smoke. In the midst of the smoke was Paul's demented smile and suddenly she saw herself being beaten relentlessly by him while he screamed at her.

On the other side of the room, Michael covered his ears trying so desperately to block out the yelling.

"What are you going to do with your life!?"

"Stop it!" Michael screamed at his father's voice.

"You're a failure!" his mother's voice was shrill. "You are nothing!"

"NO! NO! NO!" Michael's head was pounding. Every noise was amplified. Every step sounded like an infantry. Every breath sounded like a hurricane. He didn't know how much longer he could keep his eyes shut.

It was as if Zoe's identity was being stolen right out of her. Her mind was starting to go blank. Bruises and cuts began to appear on her body, blood oozed down her arms and face. Her heart began to slow. Her fingers went numb.

Suddenly, the room illuminated.

"GO!" R.L.'s voice was deep and powerful. It echoed throughout the entire circus.

Immediately at the sound of his voice, in the brightness of his light, the Shadow People vanished.

Lilly threw up the nothingness that was in her stomach, Michael and Drew ran to her aid. Jordan went to help Zoe off of the floor.

"You're okay," R.L. said. "You're okay."

Zoe tried to stand but her legs felt like jelly. She felt like she had just gotten beaten to death all over again. Jordan released her arm and was saying something to her, but his voice was muffled. She heard R.L. call her name. Then, her body went slack and she collapsed to the floor unconscious.

"Hello," Barnaby said as he sat next to Michael, Drew, and Jordan. The fire was blazing in the fireplace, but the boys still shivered. "How are you doing?"

"Better," Drew answered. Jordan nodded in agreement. Michael didn't respond, he just stared at the fire.

"Did you look at it? At the shadow?" Barnaby asked. He didn't have his clipboard with him, he didn't even have the usual pen behind his ear.

"No, but it was screaming at me, sounded just like my mom," Michael told him quietly.

"Mine was screaming, too," Jordan chimed in. Drew nodded.

"I was just starting to forget," Michael let out a frustrated sigh. "I was starting to feel better and happier, then I get dragged right back into it. It's like I'll never get away. No matter what."

Barnaby took a deep breath, "Maybe getting away isn't what you need to do, maybe getting through it is."

The boys looked at him. His voice was smooth and calm. Neither of them had ever heard him speak in such a manner.

Barnaby continued, "History is a chance to learn from mistakes. While we should not dwell on the past, we certainly should not forget. We should learn and grow and be able to look back and be proud of how far we have come. Let the past not be a reminder of what went wrong, but a guide on how to do better."

Michael nodded in agreement. The tired wheels in his head beginning to turn. "Words of wisdom, Barney," he said. Barnaby chuckled at the new nickname.

"Has Zoe woken up?" Jordan asked.

"Not yet. R.L. is waiting with her in the medical wing until she does."

Lilly sat up in the hospital bed facing where Zoe was laying in her bed still knocked unconscious. R.L. walked over and handed her a cup of tea.

"Thanks," she murmured. R.L. sat down beside her with a sad look on his face.

"Why have you not been eating, Lilly?" She nearly choked on the tea.

"I have," she tried weakly.

"You have not." She avoided his eyes as hers watered. R.L. continued, "How come? Cirque is a safe place, for you to be healthy and happy."

"I just, I look awful," she said.

"You look beautiful."

Lilly laughed at that. "You're blind then."

"I don't see the skin, I see the heart." She searched R.L.'s eyes and the fire in them comforted her. He said, "I see a strong will, a determined mind, and a compassionate heart. There are so many things that make you beautiful on the inside that without even realizing it, they leak onto the outside and make you beautiful there, too."

"Really?"

"Really." R.L. stood as nurses came in to check up on Lilly. She smiled at him, a real smile, a relieved smile.

"Thank you."

"Goodnight, Lilly."

Zoe slowly opened her eyes. R.L. was in a chair beside her with his feet propped up on the small white bed.

"Hey," he spoke softly.

She sat up and frantically checked herself for wounds.

"He wasn't actually hurting you. It was just the shadow. It was making you see those things. It was all a sick twisted illusion," R.L. explained.

"I'm sorry. I shouldn't have opened my eyes." A tear trickled down her cheek.

"It's okay—"

"It's not okay! I should've stayed strong," she yelled in frustration. "I try so hard to be but really I'm weak. My whole life I've never been able to pick myself up." She hiccupped as she tried to catch her breath. "I wish I could but I can't. I just feel so torn apart and I don't understand why it had to be me. What did I do to deserve everything I've gone through?!" Tears dripped off of her chin onto the blanket she was tightly clutching. For a moment the only sound was her sobs.

"Specifically broken," R.L.'s voice was a whisper.

Zoe sniffled. "What?"

"You are specifically broken. Torn apart for a divine purpose." He had her full attention now. "You are strong, Zoe." He took his feet down and leaned forward. "Every foul word that has ever been said to you, every disappointing look, every hit and every night you wanted to die. Every single one of those things was designed to build you into the strong wise human that you are becoming. You just need to see that you are more than capable of picking yourself up. You have never been given anything that could not be overcome."

She stared at him wide-eyed. A light hopeful feeling began to spread throughout her body. Zoe sat up straighter than she ever had before.

"That's why I'm the Contortionist." Thousands of light bulbs were going off in her mind as she spoke, "I bend but I don't break."

R.L. broke out into a huge smile. "Exactly. You are stretched but never beyond your limits." His eyes were bright with excitement. He felt as though his heart was about to burst at the sight of Zoe realizing that the way she saw herself because of all that happened to her, was really a distorted view of her strong resilient soul.

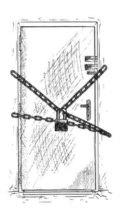

PART 3

CHAPTER 22. TENSION

R.L. sat on the edge of his mahogany desk deep in thought. Barnaby entered the office with a cup of coffee in each hand.

"Our recruits are sleeping in today." Barnaby handed R.L. his mug.

"Good. They need it after last night."

Barnaby settled himself in his usual armchair, "We have quite an interesting group this time around."

"Very interesting indeed. They're doing well though."

"Wes told me he's having slight problems with Michael. He's not following instructions too well."

"He's not a fan of authority."

"That's not good. Especially with Trapeze."

"Is everything recovered from the break-in?"

"Yes. We've doubled security as well."

R.L. nodded in approval.

"R.L., we haven't had a shadow infestation in quite some time."

"I know," Strain was visible on R.L.'s face.

"Why now? Why of all times did they choose now? What is it they want?"

R.L.'s grip on his coffee mug tightened, "The time is coming, and they want one of our new recruits."

CHAPTER 23. EKKLESIA

"Hey guys," Zoe said cheerfully as she sat down at the dining table for a late lunch.

"How are you feeling?" Michael asked her.

"Really good." They all looked at her strangely. "What?"

"You're smiling, like really smiling," Lilly said. Zoe laughed at this, surprising the group.

"It's a good day," she said. "The first good day I've had in a very, very long time." She sat up a little straighter than usual, her head held a little higher, the weight of her past a little lighter.

"And how are you, Lilly?" Drew asked. Lilly chewed her breakfast and smiled.

"Much better, I missed food."

"I'm glad," Zoe told her. "You're gorgeous. Don't need to be hurting yourself like that." Lilly nodded, embarrassed talking about it in front of the guys.

"I think I'm actually starting to like this place," Jordan said nonchalantly. Everyone raised their eyebrows at that.

Michael snorted a laugh. "It only took—wait, how long have we been here?" he asked. The group shrugged their shoulders.

"Feels like forever and one day all at once," Zoe said.

"Very poetic." Lilly giggled.

The waiters brought out their meals and they ate in comfortable silence.

"Afternoon," R.L. greeted them. "Are you all finished eating?" They nodded. "Great. Come with me, I have a surprise." He took a left from the dining hall and the group scurried after him.

"What are we doing?" Drew asked.

R.L. went through a curtain in the Commons and stopped in a short and narrow hallway where Barnaby was waiting.

"How many secret hallways does this place have?" Michael wondered aloud.

"More than we probably even know," Barnaby answered.

"Barnaby will be your escort this afternoon." R.L. put an arm around his friend's shoulders.

"Escort where?" Lilly asked.

R.L. left Barnaby's side and went to a door that blended so well into the wall none of the teenagers had even noticed it was there. R.L. smiled as he turned the knob and opened it to reveal a bustling city. They stepped outside and marveled at the world in front of them. The sky was a clear blue with a few white clouds. The breeze was warm and the streets seemed to sparkle from cleanliness.

"We're definitely not in my hometown," Jordan quipped, comparing his crumbling metro area to this perfect-looking one.

"This is the city of Ekklesia," Barnaby told them proudly.

"What country are we in?" Zoe asked. She closed her eyes and took a deep breath. She faintly smelled roasted almonds.

"We aren't," Barnaby said.

Her eyes opened in bewilderment, "What?"

"Well, have fun!" R.L. interjected. He turned and walked through the door back into the circus.

Barnaby began walking as he spoke, "I hope none of you are afraid of heights."

Drew looked to the others worriedly but they were all pre-occupied with the city around them.

People strolled along, none of them in a hurry, all of them smiling and laughing. Everyone said hello to each other, and they even greeted the group of strangers who stared at them in awe. The crowd was so diverse, none of the recruits could believe their eyes. People from every color and every background walked and laughed together. Jordan was on a search for an angry face, but he couldn't find one. There were no homeless people on the streets, no crying children, no angry nine-to-fivers. Everyone was content.

"There's no cars," Zoe observed.

"We don't need them here." Barnaby waved at a few people here and there.

"How do people get around?"

He smiled at her. "We manage." She rolled her eyes at his evasiveness.

The buildings of Ekklesia were just as varied and astonishing as the people. Steepled victorian buildings were scattered among the streets with clocks on the towers and tall windows, each building taking up half of a block. Right next to the historical architecture, were tall, high-rise buildings. Reflective on every side, they reached high into the sky. Michael rubbed his neck after craning to see how high up it went. Across the street were small-town markets, fresh fruit, and meat, newspaper stands, hot dog stands, colonial homes and downtown row houses. Brick apartment buildings next to large beautiful parks.

"I've never seen anything like this," Lilly told Zoe.

"After waking up from death in a circus tent I thought there was nothing else that

could surprise me," Zoe replied. The sun seemed to be brighter here than at home but when Zoe stared directly at it, it caused no harm to her eyes.

Drew was having flashbacks from his time behind the door of desire, it had all seemed perfect like this. He knew this wouldn't take a turn for the worse though. This city was special, it was pure. He could feel it somehow.

"Alright, here we go." Barnaby held the door open for the group as they entered a

tall narrow building that was all windows.

The lady at the large desk smiled sweetly and waved hello. Barnaby pressed the button to call the elevator that went all the way to the top of the building.

Drew gulped as he looked up.

At the dinging sound, the doors opened and they stepped into a windowed elevator. They could see the entire city, a 360° view, as they slowly climbed to the very top. All eyes went wide as they saw Cirque sitting in the very center of Ekklesia, the red and white stripes expanding wide.

"Dang, Cirque is even bigger than I thought," Michael said.

"So, we're not in a country?" Zoe crossed her arms when all Barnaby did was smile. "Is there anything that you can actually tell us about where we are, without being shady?"

"The city of Ekklesia was founded a long, long, loooooong time ago." Barnaby pressed his forehead against the glass and looked lovingly at his home. "Everyone here belongs here. It is a very happy place. A utopia if you will."

"Utopias don't exist," Michael scoffed.

Barnaby looked at him and smiled as if he knew something Michael didn't. "I suppose Cirque didn't exist to you before as well, huh?" Barnaby retorted.

"I guess," Michael mumbled.

Lilly asked, "So, is there someone in charge? A president, a King?"

"There is someone who loves everyone in this city and has made this a paradise for them to reside in," Barnaby said.

"Who?" Lilly's question went unanswered when the elevator stopped at the top of the building.

The doors opened and they hesitantly stepped out. A clear fence wrapped around the building, but it did nothing to rest Drew's twisting and turning stomach. He stayed close to the elevator and was not planning to move at all.

Barnaby went to him. "Drew, trust me, you are going to want to see this." Drew shook his head and was determined to stand firm, right where he was. But then he saw the faces of his fellow circus freaks.

No one could find the words to say as they overlooked the entirety of Ekklesia. The city was an endless beauty by itself, but it is what went beyond the city that truly stunned them. To the north, a large cobalt sea crashed onto white sandy shores. The breeze slightly carried a sea salt aroma to the group and Lilly relished in it. To the east was a wild untamed jungle. The tops of the trees varied in so many shades of green, most of which none of them had ever seen before. If they listened close enough, they could hear the calls of animals and the brushing of leaves in the wind.

To the south was a brazen desert with camels off in the distance carrying travelers. Jordan could almost feel his skin sweltering from the harsh temperature. And to the west were the thunderous snowy mountains standing amidst soft and icy white ground.

Zoe struggled to understand how these four different elements looked so close, yet the city limits seemed to span on forever.

"I don't get it." Michael ogled at the sight before him.

"You don't need to," Barnaby told him.

"Well, of course, I need to!" Michael exclaimed. "Everything here is so confusing, my head is hurting from just trying to get my thoughts in order!"

"I would think that happens to you a lot," Jordan jabbed.

Lilly piped up, "It's absolutely stunning."

"That it is. Would you like to see more?" Barnaby offered.

"Yes!" Lilly answered for everyone.

They descended to ground level and bid farewell to the woman behind the desk. As she waved, Drew noticed something on her forearm but they were outside before he could get a good look. Barnaby took them around the corner towards the town square. They walked along the sidewalks enjoying the atmosphere around them.

The balconies of the apartment buildings were covered in flowers and ivy. Children ran around with wooden swords while parents looked on laughing. Michael musically swung around the lampposts, while Lilly looked in every store window that they passed. She could practically taste the fresh bread that the baker had taken out of the oven. She could smell the hundreds of different candles, and she was very much tempted to go into the clothing store to feel the blue sweater that had looked way too soft to be real.

Jordan shook his head in disbelief as they walked. There was absolutely no way it was possible for a city to function like this.

For everyone to be friendly to everyone else, for there not to be even a single piece of trash on the street, for the roads to be perfectly paved, and the pigeons to not bug you wherever you went. Then again, there was absolutely no way it was possible to be stabbed and then come back to life in a circus, and that was happening. Although, he would argue that he still wasn't completely convinced.

"I could get used to this," Zoe said after she was greeted very kindly by a family passing by. "It's so peaceful."

They reached the town square where an enormous marble water fountain spouted glistening water. Barnaby encouraged the group to explore. Drew walked with Michael to a street vendor and as Michael pondered over his choices, Drew pointed at the man's left forearm. "What's that?" he asked while observing the tattoo of a man throwing bowling pins in the air.

"I was a juggla' back in the day." he mused proudly in his accent.

"In Cirque?" Drew asked.

"Where else?" The man handed Michael an ice cream cone. "Have a good day!"

When they got back to Barnaby, Drew pointed to the man. "That guy had a mark!" He said.

"And?" Barnaby asked.

"Why does he have a mark? What does he mean he used to be a juggler?"

"Juggla'." Barnaby and Drew ignored Michael's correction.

"Well, I believe his comment was quite simple," Barnaby said.

"Why isn't he still at Cirque?" Drew asked.

"He didn't want to be a juggler forever."

"I saw a woman with a mark, too," Drew said, remembering the woman at the desk.

"Everyone in Ekklesia is marked," Barnaby explained. "They were all once part of Cirque at one time or another." They met up with the rest of the group.

"Everyone?" Michael ate the last of his cone.

"Everyone. And now they live in Ekklesia. They chose to come back and live here. Everyone has a choice." Barnaby told them.

"So someday we could live here?" asked Jordan.

"Certainly, it all depends on you."

CHAPTER 24. INFILTRATION

"Shove a burning torch down my throat? Easy. Hold in the flames then breathe out? No problem," sarcasm dripped from Jordan's tongue.

"You know, if you put half as much energy into your art as you do your complaining you'd have mastered it by now," Annette spoke, with a hand on her hip.

"I believe in you, Jordan!" Lilly called as she walked with grace across the tightrope that stood twelve feet high.

"Ugh, alright. Let's do this." Jordan held the unlit torch out for Annette. She clicked the lighter and revealed a flame. Jordan took a deep breath.

"Focus," Annette instructed softly. "Envision the fire being inside of you. Trap it."

Jordan opened his mouth, did his best to capture the flames, and then took the torch out. A light heat coursed through his body. There was a comfortable burning in his throat.

"Count from five," Annette told him.

Jordan did as instructed and then opened his mouth releasing the flames. After a few seconds he erupted in a fit of coughs and the flames disappeared.

"Great!" Annette exclaimed. "That was amazing for your first try!"

Jordan stood stunned. He did it. He actually breathed fire. Maybe he could do this. Maybe he really was meant to be a Fire Breather.

"Let's go again." Jordan was determined to do it right. He knew he could. For the first time, he believed he could do something great.

"Are you sure? You don't want to take a break?" Annette asked.

Jordan shook his head. "I've been taking a break my whole life. I'm done. I'm ready to do this."

"Alright." Annette smiled proudly. She lit the torch.

Again they counted. This time when Jordan opened his mouth, he released a wall of blazing fire. He slowly spun in a circle, surrounding himself with flames. He opened his eyes and saw his father. He saw the concrete, he saw the buildings that had towered over him his whole life, and he saw the people that were destroying themselves bit-by-bit. He realized something as he stood among the flames.

He wasn't being burned.

There was only a soft warmth. He wasn't being affected by what surrounded him at all. The flames died down and Jordan realized that everyone had stopped what they were doing and were cheering for him.

"That was amazing!" Annette exclaimed.

"I get it," Jordan told her. His eyes were wide with understanding.

"Go ahead," she urged him to share.

"I've always been surrounded by fire, and I was letting myself burn. But I'm a *Fire Breather*. I don't have to be burned by everything around me. I don't have to become my father. I don't have to be stuck. I'm not where I come from. I can be better."

Annette had tears in her eyes as she nodded, "You are *not* a product of your surroundings." She pulled Jordan into a hug, and this time he hugged her back.

Drew expertly avoided Wyatt's jabs and even ended up unarming him.

Wyatt applauded. "Now we bring in Asier."

"What?" Drew dropped the swords.

"Don't be scared, Drew. You were—"

"Meant for this, blah, blah, blah. I still have to face a lion!"

Wyatt tried to contain his laughter. "You'll be fine."

"So beautiful child!" Alfie told Lilly when she completed the tightrope. She danced around in victory.

"I did it! I did it! I did it!" she drew out the last one as she pumped her fists in the air. Alfie laughed heartily.

"There is still much to learn," he reminded her.

"I know, I know."

"Now we will practice tricks on the rope." Alfie smiled, Lilly gulped.

Zoe copied Abrielle exactly and twisted her body into numerous positions, "Alright! What's next?" she urged.

"Geez, girl! Take a breath!" Abrielle exclaimed causing Zoe to laugh. "You're mastering this quick."

"It's different now, you know? I feel like I can do anything." Zoe looked into her trainer's eyes. She was determined, ready to take on any challenge.

"You can," Abrielle told her. "But always remember that there is always more to learn. You will continue to be stretched and pulled, but you'll adjust. You'll be fine."

"Thank you." Zoe never would have imagined being friends with someone like Abrielle, she never imagined being anything like she is now.

Abrielle responded, "You're welcome. Now, let's work on the routine."

Michael swung back and forth from the low trapezes earning a huge congratulations from Dez.

"So, when do I go to the high platform?" Michael asked out of breath. He wiped his sweaty palms on a towel.

"There is still much to learn before the high platform," Dez said.

"Aw, come on," Michael whined.

"No arguing. Now, do that again."

Michael mumbled a complaint and grabbed onto the bar, but paused when he noticed something on his skin. He watched fearfully as what looked like black ink started crawling up his left arm towards his tattoo.

"Is everything alright, Michael?" Dez called.

"Uh, yeah!" he yelled back. When he looked at his arm again there was nothing there. He couldn't help but shiver.

"Arms up," Alfie instructed Lilly. "Now slowly, one foot at a time, spin."

Lilly was back on the three-foot tightrope as she practiced 'ballerina spinning,' as Alfie called it. She was almost to the half-way mark when she remembered how her little sister took ballet classes. How she and Lilly used to dance around the living room, so carefree. And then, Lilly remembered the last party she had gone to with Maria. She remembered Damien, and she remembered going home, and she remembered dying.

"Ow!" Lilly twisted her ankle on the bar and Alfie caught her before she hit the ground.

Mia and Alfie rushed to her side.

"What happened? You were doing so good!" Milo asked. Mia helped Lilly stretch out her leg and Alfie took a look at the ankle.

"You'll be alright. With a visit to the hospital wing, you'll be fine by training time tomorrow." Alfie looked at his student. "What happened?"

"I just got distracted," Lilly played with the hem on her shirt, Mia could see the shell slowly closing around Lilly again.

"I'll take her to get a wrapping on it," Mia offered. Alfie nodded in agreement. Mia hoisted Lilly up and with her arm draped around Mia's shoulder she limped to the hospital wing.

"Hey there, girls," an older man greeted.

"Josiah, this is Lilly. Lilly, this is Josiah. He's been around since Cirque's beginning." Lilly smiled weakly as Mia introduced them. Josiah had pitch-black hair but a gray beard. Lilly marveled at how his eyes were two different colors, one a bright blue and the other forest green. Mia continued, "Lilly hurt her ankle while training."

Josiah led them over to one of the beds and Mia helped Lilly sit down. Josiah lifted Lilly's ankle up and she flinched when he did. "So sorry, dear," he said. He placed her ankle down gently. "I'll be right back."

"What happened out there, Lilly?" Mia asked. Lilly found it strange how soft she had spoken, Mia was usually loud and excited.

"I just got distracted," Lilly said quietly.

"By what?"

"Doesn't matter."

"It does matter. I'm your friend Lilly, I want to help you," Mia insisted.

"I was thinking about how I was at home, I was thinking about how I died." Lilly refused to make eye contact. Mia sat down in a chair beside Lilly. "I destroyed myself because I was so obsessed with what other people thought of me. I was a coward and I was weak. Who says I'm any different now than I was then?"

"I do. Alfie does, R.L. does. You've come a long way," Mia said.

"Not really, I still worry all the time. And now I have to perform on a tightrope with everyone watching, I'm not going to be able to do it. I'm gonna fall just like I did today." Lilly wiped her tears with the back of her hand.

"No, you won't because you won't be on that tightrope for everyone else. You're not learning one of the most dangerous arts to impress people. You're doing it to push yourself, to prove to yourself that you can do it. There will always be people who don't like you, people who think you should change.

"But then, there are people who love you exactly how you are, and those are the people you need to keep around, those are the people that matter. If you get on a tightrope, at any height, and are thinking about the people watching you, you won't ever make it to the other side. You only need to see yourself, to see your strength and your ability to do amazing things," Mia held Lilly's hand as she spoke. Lilly nodded and smiled, letting the words sink in.

"Very well said," Josiah clapped, earning a giggle from the girls. "Now Lilly, let's fix up this ankle of yours."

Michael rushed into his room and closed the door behind him. He scratched and scratched at his arms and it wasn't until he looked down that he realized what he was scratching. The skin encasing his tattoo was covered in red lines from his nails, but that wasn't what caused the sinking feeling in Michael's gut. It was the black lines that traveled up and down Michael's inner forearm.

"What the—" he said to himself. He opened the trunk at the foot of his bed and looked for a long-sleeved shirt. Why didn't he just go tell R.L. what was happening? He didn't know. He didn't realize that there was a voice whispering for him not to. He didn't see what was happening to him.

He sat on his bed a moment longer then decided to go to the Commons. He found Jordan and Zoe playing pool. Suddenly, he started feeling dizzy. He blinked over and over not believing what he was seeing. Jordan, Zoe, the couches, the chairs— everything was black and white. Michael closed his eyes and took deep breaths. He reopened them and sat down in relief, color had returned. *I should tell R.L.,* Michael thought to himself. His arm started itching again and he decided against it.

"It's awesome, it changes everything," Jordan was still in awe at his revelation as they all sat at the dinner table. The others watched him curiously, his shoulders were relaxed, he was starting conversations, he was even smiling. He noticed their stares and hardened his features. "What?" he snapped.

"Nothing," they all said with a smile.

Michael sat down and started picking at the food in front of him. He didn't even spare a glance at anyone else sitting at the table.

"You alright?" Zoe asked him.

"Fine," he responded gruffly.

"I don't know how close I am to mastering," Lilly said. "I'm starting to learn tricks and some of them are so difficult. Alfie wants me to do a cartwheel, on a rope!" Lilly threw her hands in the air dramatically causing everyone to laugh. "Why are you laughing?"

"You're so dramatic!" Zoe told her, imitating the way she constantly moved her arms. Lilly threw a pea at her and she dodged it swiftly.

"What about you, Michael?" Drew asked, trying to get him involved in the conversation.

"What?" Michael asked sharply.

"How are you doing with the trapeze?"

"Well, not as good as the rest of you of course, but you already knew that. You're just trying to make me feel worse, huh? You think you're better than me?" Michael was standing now. His world was flashing from color to black and white, his head was aching with noise, and his voice was getting louder and meaner.

"No, I didn't mean," Drew tried to defend himself.

"Whatever." Michael slammed his chair into the table and stormed off. He went up the stairs towards his room and was met with R.L. in the hallway like the Ringleader had been waiting for him.

"Michael, are you alright?" R.L. asked.

Michael battled himself internally. *Do I tell him? No, he would be mad at me. He would think there's something wrong with me.* Instead, he said, "I'm good." He tried to brush past R.L. but the Ringleader grabbed his hand as he reached for the doorknob to his bedroom door.

"Michael, are you alright?" R.L. asked again, emphasizing every word. He leaned in close and looked into Michael's eyes intensely. He was giving him another chance. A chance to tell him what was happening and allow him to help, to fix it.

"I—" Michael could feel the urgency R.L. was portraying, the Ringleader was there to help. "I'm fine. I'm just a little tired from training that's all. Good night." He pushed R.L.'s hand off and turned the knob.

He slammed the bedroom door behind him and crawled onto his bed. He held his head tightly trying to make everything stop. He closed his eyes because he couldn't stop the constant changing of color. He eventually fell asleep being haunted by nightmares and voices hissing, whispering dark negative thoughts into his mind, and filling him with fear.

CHAPTER 25. TRUST ME

"Morning!" Lilly greeted Michael as he begrudgingly sat down to breakfast. He didn't even acknowledge that she had spoken, he just stared at the plate in front of him. Drew shrugged when Lilly looked at him questioningly.

"Hey, guys." Zoe sat down beside Michael and with a slight bump spilled a glass of orange juice over. "Crap, I'm sorry."

Michael jumped up and yelled, "What is wrong with you?!"

"It was an accident," she said scooting away from him. A waiter came over with a rag and started cleaning the table.

"Way to ruin breakfast!" Michael's voice silenced the room.

"Calm down, man!" Jordan yelled as he stood to his feet.

"Don't tell me to calm down! Don't tell me anything!" They locked eyes, confusion filling Jordan's and a desperate rage filling Michael's.

"Michael," R.L.'s soft, concerned voice broke Michael's stare as he entered the dining hall.

"You either!" He pointed a finger at R.L. "Everyone, just leave me alone!" He stomped away mumbling under his breath as everyone watched in disbelief.

"What is with him?" Drew asked.

Zoe tried to steady her shaking hands. She had forgotten what it was like to be yelled at. Memories flooded her mind.

"Zoe?" R.L. rested his hand on her shoulder.

"I'm okay." She breathed in and out and within seconds her hands had stilled and her mind was brought back to the present. "I'm okay," she said again, actually meaning it for once in her life.

"I'm going to check on him, you all just resume your day. You're all excelling greatly in your training, like naturals. I'm very proud. And don't worry, I won't be saying 'I told you so.'" The group laughed and R.L. winked.

Michael didn't know where he was or where he was going. Everything was black and white, not a trace of color anywhere.

"I'm better than them," he mumbled under his breath. He moved frantically among the circus. "Dez doesn't know what he's talking about. I've already mastered the trapeze, I can go to the high platform if I want!" He scratched at his tattoo. "I don't need anyone, anyone!"

"Barnaby," R.L.'s voice was urgent. The two men met in the Commons.

"I heard about Michael's outburst," Barnaby said.

"He's being compromised, we have to find him now before things get out of hand," R.L. spoke quickly.

"I'll send out the General and tell everyone to be on the lookout."

R.L. nodded and swiftly left the office.

"Are you ready?" Wyatt asked.

Drew shook his head. They stood in the circus ring in front of a large cage that held Asier the lion. Today was the big day. The day to test out everything Drew had learned.

"Drew," Wyatt scolded.

"Fine! Fine. I'm ready." Drew took the position that Wyatt had told him to.

Shoulders back, chin up and hands folded behind his back. Wyatt opened the door to the cage and Drew entered cautiously.

Asier stood near the wall opposite Drew and looked at him menacingly. He displayed his teeth and a small rumble erupted from his chest. Drew wanted to run away so badly, but he forced himself to stay. He swallowed the lump in his throat and took slow steps toward the beast. Asier followed suit and took long strides to the novice tamer. Drew stopped in the middle of the cage and Asier continued forward. Drew raised his right hand, which was supposed to be the signal for Asier to stop, but the lion did not obey. Drew lowered his hand and raised it again, it was having no effect. Drew was letting his fear show now and he knew he wasn't ready for this, how could anyone ever be ready for this?

"Wyatt?" Drew called in an uncertain voice.

"You can do this," his instructor encouraged. He was right by the cage door just in case.

"Wyatt," Drew whined.

"Don't be scared."

"Great advice," Drew mumbled. Asier was taking his time, toying with the now sweating teenager.

Drew lifted his hand again. He could've sworn he saw Asier smile at him. *Do lions smile?* Drew's heart hammered against his chest. What was he thinking? He wasn't cut out for this, he was the biggest coward there was. He had never been brave enough or strong enough to defend himself against school bullies.

But then, a thought entered his mind and everything began to make sense.

"Wyatt," Drew's tone was different this time. Confident and sure of himself.

"Yes?" Wyatt asked, taken aback by the new tone.

"I know why I'm the Lion Tamer."

Wyatt smiled. "Good. Now show your lion why."

Drew took one more step forward and his entire demeanor changed. He wasn't a boy pretending to be a Lion Tamer anymore, he was a Lion Tamer facing his lion. He thought of every person who had ever called him names. He thought of every time he had considered ending his life. Faces of bullies flashed in his mind. Images of himself sobbing and wanting to be accepted caused his right hand to shoot up and stop Asier in his tracks. This was for all the times Drew was preyed on by lions; those days were over now.

"Down," Drew's voice rang with so much authority, it shocked *himself*. Asier laid submissively on his belly.

It was as if time stood still for a moment. All Drew could do was stare at what he had accomplished. His victory, his lion, looked at him right in the face and it seemed like a brief look of approval flash through the animal's eyes. Wyatt opened the door and Drew stepped out so very different than he first stepped in, just moments ago.

"That was unbelievable!" Drew exclaimed.

"I knew you could do it," Wyatt said proudly.

"I feel incredible. Man, I, I can't even explain it." Drew watched Asier pace inside the cage.

"Don't ever forget this feeling." Wyatt grabbed Drew by the shoulders so they were facing each other. "There's going to be days where you don't feel a trace of this courage, but you have to remind yourself that you are capable."

Drew nodded. "I am capable," he repeated to himself.

"Michael!" Everyone turned to Dez as he shouted towards the top of the circus tent. High up on the trapeze ladder was Michael, moving quickly to the highest platform. Dez ran right below the ladder and yelled, "Michael, stop! Please!"

Drew ran and stood beside Zoe who had been practicing near the lion cage.

"What is he thinking?" Drew asked. Zoe shook her head not able to find the words. Her throat grew tight with nerves.

"Michael! Please," Dez screamed again as he began climbing the ladder.

"I'm here! You two"—R.L. pointed at two of the Trapeze Artists—"get him." They ascended the ladders on either side. Dez came back to the ground and joined R.L. right beside the net. They craned their necks to see Michael moving fast.

"Michael!" R.L.'s voice cracked from the overwhelming emotions coursing through him.

Michael was so lost in his mind that he heard nothing. He saw nothing but the rungs of the ladder in front of him. He felt nothing but the desire to prove himself.

Lilly stood on one of the tightrope platforms across from Michael. He climbed up right past her. "Michael, please!" her voice was desperate. The other Trapeze Artists were climbing as quickly as they could, but Michael was still too far ahead to be stopped.

"MICHAEL!" R.L.'s scream had silenced everyone else. His eyes shined with unshed tears. "Come down, you don't need to do this. It's okay. Nobody is angry, we want to help."

Michael stepped out onto the platform and for a second, he heard R.L. He looked down at him, at everyone, and wondered why on earth he was doing this. Why was he being so stubborn? His body slightly turned to go back to the ground, but then he started scratching his arm. Voices came again. Michael obeyed them and leaped.

He grabbed onto the trapeze bar and swung himself to the next one. *I can do this,* he thought to himself. Everyone continued to scream for him. His fellow artists tried to grab him every time he swung close to the platform. Lilly even climbed the ladder to the platform across from where Michael had jumped. She was calling his name but he didn't acknowledge her pleas.

His palms were sweaty and his body was shaking. His movements on the trapeze were sloppy, dangerous to say the least. *I don't need anyone.* With that thought, Michael swung himself upward, let go of the bar, and attempted a flip towards the higher bar.

For some, it happened in slow motion, for others in a blink of an eye. For some it was loud, for others there was no sound at all. Lilly and Zoe released pained screams. Jordan and Drew stood numb.

Michael fell straight down. The net caught him, bouncing him in the air a couple of times. He blinked his eyes still in a daze. He didn't hear the people talking to him, he didn't see R.L. and the others who were running towards him. All he saw was a shadowy figure right in front of him as he sat in the middle of the trapeze net.

"Come with me," the shadow figure hissed. "I'll take you somewhere better than Cirque. A place where you rule yourself, where you answer to no one. No one to tell you what you can or can't do." The shadow crawled closer.

No one in the circus tent could see the shadow except for R.L., but Michael couldn't hear the Ringleader's shouting for him, begging him not to listen. He could only hear the alluring voice of the dark in front of him. R.L. climbed into the net, he crawled quickly towards Michael.

"We can train you far better than these fools can. They're fake, they're crazy. They're not really helping you. Not like we can help you, they don't understand you. They just want to control you!" Michael's head nodded as he listened. "Come with me, Michael. Come with me."

"Michael!" R.L. jumped forward, stretching his hands out for Michael, only an arm's length away.

Michael looked to the shadow. "Michael." The shadow figure held out its misty arm. Michael reached out his hand and as soon as he connected with the shadow he disappeared leaving behind a thick sticky cloud of black smoke.

The tent was at a standstill. No one moved, no one breathed. R.L. remained on his knees, wobbly in the net. A guttural low moan of grief came from his chest. All over the circus ring people began to weep, they held onto each other in attempts to comfort. Slowly, mechanically, R.L. made his way out of the net.

He stood now, facing the net, and stared at the ground. His eyebrows furrowed and his jaw set. Everyone watched him, waiting for him to speak, waiting for him to do something, to explain. He turned abruptly and walked out of the room.

"Hey!" Drew and Zoe followed behind a fuming Jordan as he yelled. Lilly ran to catch up to the group. "HEY!" Jordan yelled again, the veins on his neck threatened to burst. R.L. turned to him. "You said nothing bad would happen to us here!" Jordan poked R.L.'s chest. His hand was trembling.

"Unless it was brought on by yourselves," R.L. told him. He turned and continued walking.

"What? So Michael wanted to die? Again?" Zoe said emphatically as she stomped beside Jordan.

"He's not dead," responded R.L. They walked through the Commons.

"What?" the teenagers said together.

R.L. turned to them so fast Jordan and Zoe stumbled back. "Michael is not dead," he spoke quickly, fiercely. "He has been captured and I have to get him back before it is too late." His eyes burned a brighter orange than any of them had ever seen. "We are our own worst enemies. When pride, doubt, and fear cloud our minds, it drives us to do things we wouldn't normally do. Michael was overcome by doubt! Fear! And pride!" He took a step back. "And *that* is what led to his capture." He adjusted his top hat that had gone crooked while he spoke.

"Who took him?" Lilly asked.

"The Shadows," the Ringleader growled. He clenched his fists in anger.

"The Shadows? They're back? What if they take the rest of us?" Zoe shrieked in fear. R.L. put his hand on her shoulder to steady her shaking.

His voice softened, "It is not the Shadows we must fear, it is ourselves. It is the thoughts in our heads that lead to our downfall. Thoughts of inferiority. We have to make the choice, every single day to see the light. We have to choose to see the beauty in the world rather than the chaos. We have to choose to believe that we are strong enough, that we are worth it. The Shadows look for any tiny crack in our armor to slip through. We cannot let them take hold of us. I couldn't make the choice for Michael, it is one he had to make on his own." R.L. started up the stairs towards the Hall of Choice. The group began to follow but he stopped them. "I must do this alone."

"But—" Drew started to protest.

"Trust me." The group nodded and R.L. closed the door behind him.

Lilly, Drew, Zoe and Jordan sat at the marble top island in the middle of the kitchen. The circus was tense. People were barely talking. Everyone was just waiting, all worried about the outcome of their funny Trapeze Artist. Amelia sat glasses of milk in front of each teenager and plates of desserts as well.

"What if R.L. can't save him?" Drew stared into his milk. He had been surprised by the desire he had to follow R.L. wherever he had gone. The newfound courage to do battle, to fight off the Shadows and save Michael.

"He can," Amelia said at once. "He can do anything."

Jordan cracked his knuckles anxiously. He hadn't had cigarette cravings in so long but the familiar irritable feeling was coming back to him. He was angry. *No one messes with my family,* he thought, caught off guard by the thought. He looked around him. These strangers, these people, they were family now. Michael, as annoying as he could be, was family. He needed to do something, he hated just sitting here feeling useless.

"You must have a lot of faith in him," Zoe said, breaking Jordan from his thoughts.

"I do." Amelia leaned on the counter across from the group.

"Why?" Drew felt his own doubt threatening to creep in. He had trusted R.L. and had fallen for this scheme, and now what? One of their own was gone.

"He's proven it to me, over and over again. Just like he has to you all," Amelia's voice was steady, not a trace of disbelief.

"He hasn't proven anything except that we're not safe here like he promised we would be," Zoe spat angrily.

"He saved you." Amelia gently set her hand on top of Zoe's. The chef spoke softly. "He saved all of you, but he won't just flip a switch and make everything happen perfectly. We're not robots, we're human and things happen. Michael let the wrong things in, but there is always another chance."

"I don't understand," Zoe groaned. She put her head down on the counter. Amelia stroked her hair softly. Zoe closed her eyes and remembered when her mother used to do that when she was little before her dad left. An involuntary tear rolled down her nose.

"We aren't made to understand everything," Amelia said. "Believe you me, I've had my moments of not understanding but I have decided not to live a life of if-only's, but rather a life of even-if's."

"Meaning what?" Drew asked.

"Meaning, that when everything goes wrong I won't say 'if only' I had done this, or 'if only' that person had been there, or 'if only' this hadn't happened to me.' Instead, I will say 'even if' this or that happens, 'even if nothing goes the way I wish it would, I can overcome it. I am strong. I am not a victim and I have people watching out for me.' So, in this situation, I say, even if Michael doesn't return to us, R.L. is true to his word. He is trying everything to get Michael back. He cares about you, about all of us, and your time at Cirque won't lose its meaning."

CHAPTER 26.

TWISTED CIRCUS

Everything about the city was dark. The sky, the buildings, the dirty streets. It was cold, a burning frostbitten kind of cold. Michael blinked and rubbed his eyes over and over but realized that his surroundings were all black and white.

The breeze blew trash among the barren streets. The city looked like it had been abandoned for years. For every standing building, there were four completely destroyed ones. The streets looked like they had been through a terrible natural disaster.

Michael stumbled throughout the city looking for a way out.

"Cirque," he mumbled. "I need to get to Cirque."

Lightning lit up the sky and blinded Michael. Thunder shook the earth causing him to fall to his knees. After a moment, the city was once again deathly still. Michael saw a light coming from a small house up ahead. He crawled forward until he had enough strength to walk again. His arms and legs felt like jelly.

He gripped the stair railing tightly and pulled himself up to the front door. He knocked but there was no answer. He turned the knob and pushed it open. Classical music greeted him when he stepped into a very familiar living room. He stood staring at his mother's retreating figure as she went into the kitchen. He stepped slowly through the archway and saw his father and brother sitting at the dining room table. Both men looked at Michael with disgust.

"Aren't you supposed to be dead?" Christopher scoffed at his son. Michael remained silent.

Robby stood. "You should've stayed dead." Michael tripped over his own feet while backing away from his brother. Robby towered hauntingly over him. "We don't want you here!" Robby took another step forward and Michael took off running.

He fell down the last couple of steps and ran as fast as he could down the desolate streets. He heard Robby following him, he turned down another street and the sound of an engine revving up echoed against the brick walls. He turned to his right and saw a black Cadillac with its headlights shining right on him. As for the driver, all Michael could see were tiny white slits where eyes should have been. After revving the engine one more time, the car lurched forward speeding towards Michael. Determined not to end up as roadkill again, Michael took off.

The car turned sharply following right behind him. There was no way he was going to outrun the sadistic driver. He made a sharp turn down a narrow alleyway that smelled like an animal had died. When he came out on the other side he was in what looked like an empty parking lot. He shivered as the rain poured down on him and he stuck his hands in his pockets to try to warm them up. In the distance, he could hear the roar of the car and the squealing of the tires on the wet pavement.

Straight ahead he saw a single light hovering over a large puddle that filled a hole in the blacktop. He could feel the warmth of the light from where he stood, the distance didn't make a difference. The closer he got to the light the more he needed it, the more his mind urged him to take hold of it. Finally, he stood right in front of the light. His sneakers were soaked as he stood in the puddle, but he couldn't feel the chill that assaulted his toes. He couldn't feel anything except the comfort coming from the orb in front of him. He reached out to grab it. He reached, and reached, and then, smack!

Michael landed flat on his face. He groaned as he hoisted himself up. He froze mid-rise when slow mechanical music began to play. It sounded like it was supposed to be whimsical, but it was out of tune and too slow to be enjoyable. Michael sat on his knees and felt his stomach drop as he looked around.

Black and white stripes surrounded him and met each other in a point a hundred feet above his head. Empty, half-destroyed bleachers sat in a circle around the center where he currently was. Ripped posters hung from the ceiling. The faces of the performers scratched out with long jagged stripes and their names covered with spray-painted insults. *Lion Lamers.* A red *L* covered the original *T* in *Tamers* and a bad handlebar mustache was sprayed onto the tamers face in the poster. *Masters of the Trapeze* was completely crossed out and replaced with *Flying Monkeys* in bold black letters. Each act was defaced and demeaned with corny words and horrible illustrations.

"Ladies and gentlemen," an abnormally deep voice filled the tent. The voice sent chills down Michael's spine. "Boys and girls." Smoke began to rise up from the ground. "Screw-ups of all ages." Michael stood up trying to see who was speaking. "Tonight I have stolen you away. I have invaded your mind, your heart, your dreams. Despair will materialize right before your very eyes," the voice let out a menacing chuckle. It held malice and evoked fear. "Here at *this* Circus, we don't believe in you! We don't care about you!"

The voice got louder, "There is no such thing as extraordinary, no such thing as special! Tonight and forever you will experience pain and hopelessness! You are now where you belong—where you've always belonged. You are no good, you are worthless. This is where you deserve to be. You are now entering a place from which you will never get to leave." The dark voice rung out his last word. Reality began to sink in. Michael had been taken by the Shadows and now, he was stuck here.

"It is my pleasure and my privilege." The lights went out completely. "To welcome you." Dozens of manic voices erupted in laughter. "To Cirque." The tent went dead silent. "De La Mort." The only sound was Michael's own panicked breathing.

He screamed as the top of the circus tent lit up and startled him. Figures came flying down one after another standing straight up around him. Stomping people came into the tent so loud it hurt Michael's ears. They all said his name over and over again. Horrible music was playing, screeches and roars from animals got closer and closer. Michael lifted his head up and through a crack in the crowd around him, he saw a hallway. He needed to get back to that rainy city, anywhere would be better than this twisted circus.

He counted to three in his head and then took off as fast as he could towards the hallway. He could hear those creatures coming after him. He ran down the hallway and almost tripped a couple of times from the cracked uneven floor. There were no doors in the hallway. There was no way out. He just kept running, hoping the hall would lead somewhere.

Yells and shouts were following behind him and getting louder by the second. He didn't know how much longer he had. His legs throbbed in pain, and he feared he wouldn't be able to stand much longer. His chest hurt from running and from how hard he was breathing. He squinted his eyes, trying to make out what was in front of him. Light. It was the same light that got him here. He pushed himself even further, desperate to get out. Everything shook as the stampede of Shadows charged after him. With a final burst of energy, Michael jumped into the ball of light hoping he would end up in the city.

He landed in a muddy puddle. The light vanished from behind him and he was left alone in the empty parking lot once again. He wiped his scraped palms on his jeans and stood up. In front of him, he saw a tall brick building and an open door. Michael figured he needed a place to rest, he needed a place to hide. The building was leaky and crumbling. The staircase going up was missing the middle steps so Michael opted for going down instead.

As soon as he descended the stairs, he was assaulted with harsh voices. Hands grabbed at Michael pulling him this way and that. Lightning struck illuminating the room he was in and Michael screamed at all the skeletal figures surrounding him. Thunder boomed and shook the staircase causing Michael to go plummeting to the ground below.

R.L. stood in the Hall of Choice and sifted his keyring out of his pocket. He went to the tall black metal door and began unlocking the several locks that kept it closed. R.L. shut the door behind him and locked it. He couldn't have anyone else coming in or anything getting out.

"You would've been a terrible Trapeze Artist," the Shadows whispered to Michael.

He trembled in fear. He couldn't see a thing. It was too dark, no matter how hard he tried to adjust his vision. He furiously scratched his arm as he ran.

"You are nothing!"

"You don't matter!"

"Stop it!" he screamed at the voices.

"You're no different from anyone else."

"What purpose do you serve?"

"Please, stop!" he begged.

"No one cares that you're gone."

"Shut up! Shut up!"

Michael was in his right mind now. The moments leading up to his fall kept replaying. He heard his name being screamed. His friends, everyone trying to help him— but he hadn't let them. The black ink had covered both his arms by now, and his neck started to itch. He had chosen the shadow. He had chosen this twisted circus over Cirque. What had he been thinking?

"No," he murmured. "No, no, no!"

He continued running, looking for a way out.

"There's no way out." The voices laughed at him.

"You'll be one of us soon," they whispered. He heard metal clanking sounds like prison cell doors being slammed closed over and over again.

"No!" Michael screamed at them.

R.L. ran towards Michael's voice. He was surrounded by darkness. The Shadows fled from R.L. He knew he had to work fast and find Michael now before it was too late.

Michael had never been so scared in his life. He had never felt so guilty either. He had let everyone down. Dez, R.L., his friends—himself.

"They're happy to be rid of you. Nobody likes a smart ass," a voice told him.

It was as if Michael was running with his eyes closed. He let out a tired angry scream and fell to the floor. He cried like he had never cried before. His body shook with great sobs of utter hopelessness, his face soaked with liquid loneliness.

He coughed, tried to catch his breath, and he managed a mangled whisper, "R.L. Please, please, help." He sobbed again, his body trembling with despair.

Suddenly, the darkness stopped its whispering. Instead, there were panicked cries in the distance, as if they were worried about something coming their way. Michael heard distant footsteps that he recognized immediately. *No way,* he thought to himself. *It couldn't be. He wouldn't come for me. No one would come for me.* He curled up in a ball.

R.L. could hear the voices, then he heard Michael's broken sobs. The Shadows tried to keep him from getting to Michael, but R.L. simply brushed them aside. His hand caused a glittery red glow to break apart their black mist.

"Michael," R.L. boomed when he saw him lying in the fetal position. Michael didn't look up. R.L. knelt down. "Michael"— he grabbed his shoulders and shook him—"Michael!"

"You're not real!" Michael shouted. He was too lost in his own torment to recognize his savior.

"I am real, Michael. I'm here. I came for you." R.L. explained quickly.

"No." Michael shook his head and sobbed. He was in so much pain.

R.L. sat him up and cried at what he saw. Michael's arms were covered, his tattoo was completely black, the same color as his eyes. The ink was slithering up his jaw.

R.L. pressed his thumbs firmly into the inside of Michael's wrists. The ink began to disappear from Michael's neck. The color returned to his eyes and he saw R.L.

"It is you," Michael gasped.

The flames in R.L.'s eyes burned red. Michael looked down to see what was happening. The color was starting to return to his arms, the ink was leaving and going into R.L.'s arms.

"No!" Michael yelled, trying to get out of R.L.'s grasp. He wouldn't allow someone else to suffer because of his own stupidity.

"It's okay," R.L. stammered. Michael could tell he was in pain. R.L. continued to take all the hurt, all the despair, straight from Michael.

"It's hurting you," Michael cried.

"I'd rather that than for it to hurt you." Eventually, there was not a trace of black ink on Michael's skin. R.L. had taken it all.

"Now it's on you though," Michael said.

R.L. shook his head. "It can't hurt me the way it hurts you. Let's get out of here." Michael untangled himself from R.L.'s grasp.

"No, no, no, I can't go back," Michael told him.

"Why not?"

"I messed up, I'm weak. I don't belong there. I might as well just stay here."

"No!" R.L. yelled. "You have every right to be back in Cirque. The past is past, don't let it ruin the future."

"But, I messed up," Michael insisted.

"And?"

Michael stared at the Ringleader. "And I let you down."

R.L. stood up and reached out his hand. "It is your choice, Michael. But with me, there is a world of second chances awaiting you."

The Shadows screamed in fury and Michael cringed at their sharp voices. He grabbed onto R.L.'s arm. "You! I choose you!" he yelled.

They pushed through the darkness. Their clothes were being pulled at and a patch of ice began to spread beneath them.

"Almost there," R.L. called out to Michael as they ran.

They reached the door to Cirque and R.L. was quick to unlock all the locks. Michael could feel whatever it was they had been running from getting closer and closer. R.L. hurriedly turned the keys. Michael heard laughing. He turned his head and saw the white slits again. R.L. yanked Michael into the hallway and slammed the door shut, sealing it.

"What was that thing?" Michael couldn't stop his hands from shaking. R.L. shook his head.

"It was nothing to worry about. You're safe—you're home."
He helped Michael off the floor.

Michael took deep breaths and looked at the Ringleader.
R.L. smiled at him and before Michael could talk himself out of
it, he wrapped his arms around R.L. and hugged tight. "Thank
you," he said. R.L. hugged him back.

"Of course," R.L. told him. "You're okay now." Michael
nodded and took a step back. "Come, I'm sure everyone is eager
for your return."

By the time they entered the Commons, Michael's shaking had died down to slight shivering. Everyone was gathered
together, anticipation and worry evident on their faces. Smiles
and cheers broke out as they walked in and everyone shouted their welcomes. R.L. helped push him through the crowd
to where his fellow freaks stood. Amelia came and wrapped a
blanket around Michael's shoulders. They led him to sit on the
couch in front of the fire and they sat around him.

Drew squeezed his shoulder. "We were worried." Michael
looked at Drew to make sure he had heard right. He then looked
at Jordan who sat next to him, he nodded and smiled.

"You idiot," Zoe hit him upside the head and then smiled
softly. "You scared us."

"I'm glad you're okay!" Lilly pulled him into a tight hug.

Michael laughed breathlessly. "Man, I need to disappear
more often." Lilly nudged him with her elbow and joined Zoe
to sit on the rug.

Michael recounted the twisted circus to his friends as they sat in the glow of the fireplace. They couldn't help but shiver in disgust. He left out some descriptions, not ready to relive it all just yet.

"Michael!" Dez cried. Michael stood and turned to his instructor shamefully.

"I'm sorry Dez, I should've listened to you—"

Dez hugged him. "Yes, you should've, but you're here and you're okay, that's what's important."

"I'm ready to do this now, to really do it," Michael told him urgently.

"Good. Tomorrow we will work, tonight you will rest," Dez gave him another hug.

Michael nodded in agreement.

Music had begun to fill the room and Cirque was breaking out into a celebration. The musicians from the Side Show had set up shop and there was already a crowd on the dance floor. The group looked around for R.L. and didn't see him anywhere.

"Barnaby, where's R.L.?" Zoe asked.

"He's probably in his office," Barnaby answered.

"Where's his office?" Lilly asked.

"Follow me." Barnaby turned and began walking away.

R.L. sat in his chair with his eyes closed and his head leaned back.

"R.L.?" Michael gently knocked on the half-open door.

R.L. motioned for them to come in.

"I don't understand," Michael said, "what happened to me? Where was I? What were we running from? What—"

"Okay." R.L. put his hands up to stop the questions.

Michael looked at his hands and winced, remembering the black ink filling the Ringleader's hands.

R.L. spoke slowly, "You were overtaken by Shadows. The night they attacked they must have latched on. They were feeding you lies, preying on your insecurities in an attempt to destroy you. They took you to their home."

"Why is their home in Cirque?" Drew asked.

"Because whether they realize it or not they are subject to me. They say to 'keep your enemies closer'. When they do seep into Cirque they are always taken care of."

"Can they get into the city, too? Into Ekklesia?" Lilly asked.

"No. They cannot step foot into the city or they turn to dust. They can only enter into Cirque and into your world. Believe it or not, Cirque is not perfect. Even with so much good, the Shadows manage to creep in, the same as in your world."

"Really?" Zoe and Drew asked together in disbelief.

"You've been around the Shadows your entire lives. They are just a lot easier to see here at Cirque," R.L. said.

They were silent for a moment thinking that through.

"How did you take all that stuff from me?" Michael whispered. He rubbed his wrists remembering.

"It's what I do, Michael. I help people."

"But it hurt you," Michael said, feeling guilty.

"It's okay. I'm okay." R.L. smiled.

"Are you the hero?" Lilly spoke.

R.L. looked at her.

Lilly continued, "The story that Clyde told us. Was it true? The hero that defeated the Evil, the Shadows. Were you, are you, the hero that everyone loved?"

The look in the Ringleader's eyes revealed the truth. Jordan shot up out of his chair.

"If you're the hero that's been around forever wanting to help everyone that ever lived, then why weren't we brought to Cirque sooner? Why did you wait 'til we were all dead to help us? Huh? Why'd you wait 'til we were out of life to change it? Why'd you wait so damn long?" Jordan's voice cracked as he screamed.

R.L. stood up and slammed his hands on his desk. "I have been trying for years, Jordan!" he matched Jordan's volume, his voice was desperate. Jordan was taken aback. "You wouldn't listen, none of you would listen! I screamed your name day after day trying to get you to hear, to see," his voice cracked with emotion, his eyes watering with tears, "it pained me to watch as you all continued living the lives you were. I wanted nothing more than for you to come with me to Cirque but all of you were too lost, too focused on everything going wrong. I tried Jordan, I tried, but it wasn't until your last breath that you let down your walls and allowed me in."

Tears soaked his cheeks and his chest heaved. Jordan didn't bother wiping his own eyes, none of them did.

R.L. told them, "I chose you all a long time ago, but it had to come down to you choosing me."

Lilly got up from her chair and went to the Ringleader. She wrapped her arms around him and cried into his chest.

"Thank you," she whispered. He rubbed her back. He looked at Jordan.

Jordan nodded his head. "Yeah," he choked out.

They stood there like that, for how long, none of them could say. There was something in that room that none of them could explain. But to know that someone had been looking out for them, that someone had been trying to help—to know that someone had been crying and hurting with them all those years—that was something that changed everything.

PART 4

CHAPTER 27. YOU'RE READY

"You're ready." Alfie nudged Lilly to the edge of the tallest platform in the circus ring and then stepped back beside R.L. She stood with the rope stretched out before her. Her body was trembling. She looked down to see almost everyone watching her. She saw the other walkers looking up. She stepped back and shook her head.

"I can't, I can't do it. I,I—" Lilly stammered.

"Lilly." Alfie put his hands on her shoulders. "You can."

"They're all watching, I'm gonna fall," she whispered to him.

"Listen to me, when you're on this tightrope, *you* are the only thing keeping yourself from falling. And when you're 200 feet above the ground, no one cares what you look like or what you're wearing or who you're friends with. They care about whether or not you are going to have enough faith in yourself necessary to make it to the other side."

"But I'm the person with the least faith in myself," she hung her head low.

"If that were true, you would not have been marked as a Tightrope Walker," Alfie said firmly.

Lilly looked at the rope once more.

"You *can* do this Lilly. You have what it takes. This walk you're about to take is all about you, it's about proving to *yourself* exactly who you are."

She turned away from Alfie and toward the rope. "You're right," she said. She took a step forward and not once did she look back.

Two cartwheels and three pirouettes later, everyone applauded as she stood laughing and crying on the other side of Alfie and R.L.

"I did it!" she squealed.

That feeling inside of her was one she never wanted to lose. As she danced around as an official Tightrope Walker, she didn't think about how she purged herself, the meaningless sex that left her empty, or how she felt unworthy. All she could think about was the fact that she made it to the other side. That's all that mattered.

The Fire Breathers marched together and Jordan stood in the middle of the group, shooting fire up out of his mouth so high it almost burned the tent ceiling. Zoe was effortlessly folded into a box, and Drew and Asier played their game of cat and mouse with Drew always winning. Michael swung gracefully from bar-to-bar and person-to-person.

Dez clapped proudly. "You're ready for the high platform," he told him.

"You really think?" Michael didn't try to contain his excitement.

"I really do." Michael jumped Dez with a hug, earning a laugh and a nudge for him to get off.

Michael climbed the ladder, a flashback of the last time entering his mind. He shook it out and knew that he was okay now; R.L. had made sure of that. He stood on the platform and looked at the ground so far below him. He looked at the trapeze bar in front of him

"Michael?" Dez climbed up behind him. "Everything okay?"

"I think I know why I'm a Trapeze Artist," Michael said slowly, the pieces coming together in his head. "I've been lost, my entire life. I had everything planned out, but not by me. I didn't know who I was or what I wanted. I didn't know where to go so I just didn't go anywhere. But as a Trapeze Artist, you have to jump. You have to take a chance, you have to have faith," Michael began talking faster as excitement grew inside of him, "so maybe it's okay that I don't know exactly what the future looks like, as long as I leap towards it. I can't let my family tell me who I am or who I'm not. That's something I decide. And, there will always be a net to catch me if I fall."

Dez smiled, "I'm very proud of you, Michael."

Michael never thought he would hear that sentence said to him.

The group sat at dinner laughing and teasing and telling story after story. R.L. watched in awe at the teenagers that sat at the table, so different from the first night they arrived. A slight pang was felt in his chest; he knew that it was almost time.

"You're all exceptionally hyper tonight," Barnaby observed when he approached their dinner table.

"It's a good night," Michael told him. The others nodded in agreement.

"Well, tomorrow night will be far greater," Barnaby said as he sat down.

"What's tomorrow night?" Drew asked.

"Your performance," Barnaby answered. Zoe choked on her soda.

"What?" Jordan asked.

"Tomorrow, Cirque will be performing in front of our audience. You are all a part of Cirque, therefore, you will be performing," Barnaby spoke with a smile. He noticed their expressions. "Why do you look scared? You are masters, you are going to be phenomenal." After Barnaby left, they all looked at each other in shock.

"That's like thousands of people. When we first got here we saw Cirque perform and there were like *thousands* of people!" Lilly whisper yelled.

"I don't know, I'm not too worried," Michael said.

"Yeah." Drew shrugged his shoulders. "We've all mastered our trades. We'll be fine."

"I guess." Lilly stopped tugging on the hem of her shirt as bits of confidence began to fill her. Zoe left the table without a word.

R.L. found her sitting in the Big Top on the bleachers, staring up at the poster of the Contortionists.

"I don't know if I can do it tomorrow," she told him.

"And why is that?" He sat next to her.

"I'm not sure, something just feels wrong. It's like something is—I don't know." She hung her head.

"As if something is holding you back."

She looked in his eyes. "Yeah."

"I may know what it is."

"You definitely do. You know everything."

"That is true." R.L. chuckled.

"Well?"

"You're still very angry at your stepfather," R.L. told her gently. Zoe clenched her fist and felt her face heat up in anger.

"Well duh! How can I not be?!" she exclaimed.

"You have every right to be angry, but it's what's holding you back," R.L.'s calm tone was a stark contrast to Zoe's loud defensive one.

"How am I supposed to not be angry with him?!"

"Forgive." Even though R.L. whispered it softly, the single word still hit Zoe in the gut. Hard.

Zoe was standing up now facing away from R.L. Her voice echoed in the empty tent, "Are you freaking kidding me?! You expect me to forgive the man who made my life a living hell? The man who *killed* me!?"

"It won't be easy, but it will be worth it."

"He doesn't deserve forgiveness!"

"But *you* do," R.L. said. Zoe was silent. "Anger eats us up Zoe, from the inside until there is nothing left. You know that first hand." He reached out for her hand and led her to sit down next to him. "Forgiveness does nothing for the other person, but it does everything for you." She looked in his eyes as he spoke, hating every word he said. "It gives *you* peace, it gives you the ability to move on."

"It's hard."

"And it is not something that happens overnight. It might take years to fully forgive him, but you must start. Otherwise, he ends up winning." Zoe's eyes hardened at that. "Because for the rest of your life you will be consumed with your anger towards him. He'll still be controlling you and hurting you unless you allow yourself to let go."

They sat quietly, R.L. allowing her to process and digest the difficult task he just laid before her. Zoe's eyes flitted back and forth as she thought. She replayed R.L.'s words in her mind. She thought about how Paul really did control her, even when he wasn't around. *Do I really wanna live like that forever?* She shook her head. *No, I don't. And I won't.*

She looked at R.L. and spoke, "Thank you. Thank you for not hurting me. Thank you for keeping me safe. Thank you for helping me disprove my theory that all men are evil," Zoe chuckled nervously.

R.L. hugged her. "Thank you for being you and allowing me to help. You're going to be more than okay, Zoe."

She nodded and smiled, believing it.

R.L. stood. "Now come, there is one more thing I must show you and the others." They made their way to the Hall of Choice where the rest of the group waited with Barnaby.

R.L. spoke to the group, "Since your stay here almost every one of these doors has been opened." He gestured to the six doors.

"Yeah, sorry about that." Drew chuckled.

"No worries, you know what they say about curiosity," R.L. said.

"It killed the cat?" Michael offered.

"No, no, it gave him wings." R.L. turned to the broken, decayed looking door. He took a deep breath. "Curiosity leads us places. To adventures, dreams, passions. These doors were meant for you to open. And this door, the Door of Need, is the most important door in all of Cirque."

He unlocked it and gently pushed it open. The group stepped into a circular room with the only illumination coming from the floor. The room was plain causing all attention to be drawn to five tall silver rectangular cases that stood in a semi-circle a few feet away from each other.

"Go ahead." The Ringleader stepped aside.

Not until taking a few steps toward the cases did the teenagers realize that there were translucent markings on each of them matching the markings on their arms. Lilly traced the mark of the Tightrope Walker on a case causing it to open. Inside was a light pink leotard with gold sequins adorning the long sleeves. It was coupled with the shoes Alfie had given her.

She turned to R.L. and asked, "This is for me?"

R.L. nodded.

Just then, the other cases opened. Jordan felt the fireproof black material of his outfit. A thick strapped muscle tank top, pants, and boots. Michael laughed as he saw the clothing before him, knowing that before Cirque he wouldn't be caught dead wearing the navy blue bodysuit with silver swirls up and down the arms and legs. Zoe smiled as she took her suit off of the hanger and held it close to her; the white spandex material with black stripes just above the wrists and ankles.

"We wear these tomorrow?" Drew asked R.L. without looking at him. His eyes were captivated by the blazer that hung before him. Red lines stood boldly against the black as they ran from the neck to the shoulder where gold tassels hung. He had never owned anything so fancy.

"You do. You've earned these." R.L. smiled proudly.

"Thank you," Jordan told him.

"Wow, you didn't even mumble," Michael commented.

Jordan rolled his eyes.

"You've all come a long way," R.L. mused, "you were a lot different when you first came to Cirque than you are now. You were angry and hurt and confused and sad. You were letting the world, which doesn't know the first thing about living, tell you how to live." Memories flooded the minds of the five that stood before R.L. "But what I see now, are strong, brave, free individuals. Those garments are your rightful clothes. Those marks on your arms set you apart, they let everyone know that you belong to something bigger than yourselves. Something great. They are a reminder that you have a purpose, a reason to live, and a call to live a meaningful life."

A celebration was in order, according to Barnaby, and the group was escorted to the Commons where all of Cirque gathered. Music blasted and people danced, the Side Show performers brought all sorts of life to the party.

"Hey!" Gina approached Michael, Jordan and Drew with a big smile. "Congrats on being official!" They clinked their glasses together causing the light blue liquid to swish.

"What exactly is this?" Jordan asked.

"Comes straight from the Ekklesia springs, up in the mountains."

"So, it's just water?" Michael deadpanned.

"Try it and see."

The boys all looked to each other before bringing the goblets to their mouths.

"Woah," Drew said in response. Whatever kind of water it was he had never tasted anything so refreshing and thirst-quenching in his life.

Gina laughed, "Are you guys ready for tomorrow?"

"I think so," Jordan answered.

"I remember how nervous I was my first performance night. Aw man, I almost threw up at how scared I was," she recalled.

"Really?" Michael could hardly believe that the girl sporting weaponry would be scared of anything.

"Yeah, I remember thinking about how mortified my mother would be if she saw me shooting a gun."

"How did you end up at Cirque?" Drew questioned.

"Same way you did," she said.

"You died?"

"In a sense. I was in a deep depression. I had given up on everyone and everything. I was a walking corpse. But then R.L. brought me here."

"So, we're not the first people to come here like this?"

"Of course not. And you won't be the last. It's a legacy, one that was here before any of us and one that will last into eternity. A legacy that you are all a part of now."

CHAPTER 28. SHOWTIME

Music played in the Big Top as the citizens of Ekklesia entered and took their seats. Children, still reeling from seeing all of the oddities in the Side Show, were just seconds from combustion as they sat in the bleachers impatiently waiting for the circus to begin.

"Cotton candy! Get your cotton candy!"

"Popcorn! Popcorn! Popcorn!"

"I've got light-up crowns! Light-up wands! Light-up swords!"

Cirque's performers waited backstage behind the thick curtain listening to the excited commotion happening just beyond them.

"I am freaking out," Zoe told Abrielle. She paced back and forth shaking her hands wildly trying to release the jitters that were built up inside her.

"You're gonna be fine," Abrielle told her for the millionth time.

"I'm gonna freeze out there. Oh no, what if I get a cramp?!"

"Zoe! Sit down and chill. You're psyching yourself out." Abrielle tried not to laugh at Zoe's nervous face. She scrunched up Zoe's cheeks and enunciated, "You are going to do great. Okay?"

Zoe nodded and took deep breaths.

"R.L., you're up in two!" Barnaby spoke. He stood on a platform above all the performers with his clipboards and pens. Before going into the Big Top, R.L. gathered his newest freaks.

"You're all going to do amazing out there. You've earned tonight. You've earned the spotlight, the applause, the satisfaction. Bask in it, know that you have overcome and that you will always overcome." They nodded and R.L. brought them into a group hug. "One more thing," R.L. said and pointed behind the group. They turned towards Barnaby who stood a few feet away and held an empty rectangular gold picture frame in front of him.

"Smile," Barnaby said. They did as they were told but were confused as to what he was doing. Sparks went off like a flash and within a second the group's picture filled the once empty frame.

"How in the world did you do that?" Michael asked.

"Time to start the show!" Barnaby announced.

"Ladies and gentlemen," R.L.'s voice filled the Big Top. "Boys and girls." Lilly squeezed Zoe's hand. "Children of all ages." Michael asked Barnaby if he could get cotton candy. "It is my pleasure and my privilege." Drew peeked through a small opening in the curtain and regretted it when he saw all the people. "To welcome you all." Jordan stood with Annette's arm wrapped around his own. "To Cirque Des Élus!" The band played as lights flashed in all different colors and the audience stood to their feet cheering.

"Trapeze to the platforms!" Barnaby ushered Michael and his fellow Trapeze Artists up to their platforms.

"Good luck, Michael!" Lilly called.

Michael climbed up the ladder and tried not to look down.

"I can do this," he told himself.

R.L.'s voice bellowed, "Feast your eyes to the sky!"

The Trapeze Artists were illuminated and once the music started and Michael took his first leap, he thought of nothing but his capability. The audience gasped and clapped and stood to their feet in amazement as Michael jumped from the high platform, performed his flips perfectly and grabbed onto the arms that were stretched out for him. R.L.'s chest swelled with pride as he watched on.

"You did great, man." Jordan clapped him on the shoulder once he was back on the ground. Michael was too out of breath to respond. Barnaby handed him a towel and offered congratulations before sending Jordan off.

"With no protection between them and the flame, I present, the Fire Breathers," R.L. stepped out of the way as the group in black stomped their way to the middle of the tent.

Jordan lit the silver-handed torch and tossed it from left to right, right to left, left to right. He then stole the show as he released an endless flame of fire from his mouth. He took his bow and gave Annette a hug when he returned backstage.

"Thank you," he told her. She hugged him back knowing that he needed it far more than he would ever admit.

"It's going great, everyone," Barnaby encouraged as the elephants paraded around the arena, "Next up is Contortionists. Get ready."

"Oh no," Zoe dropped her head in her hands.

"Let's go," Abrielle grabbed Zoe. "You've got this," she told her.

"I've got this," Zoe repeated. The Contortionists made their way to the platforms.

"This next act will leave you doubting that these people have any bones at all," The spotlight momentarily blinded Zoe but she quickly adjusted her eyes. She placed her hands on her hips and dug her fingers into her skin out of nervousness. "See and believe—the Contortionists!" The chime sounded and Zoe took a deep breath.

"You're doing wonderful," Abrielle whispered as they began folding Zoe into the box after dragging her around like a rag doll. The crowd whooped and hollered as they helped Zoe out and the Contortionists took their bows.

When they got off stage Abrielle wrapped her arms tightly around Zoe and sniffled.

"What is it?" Zoe asked.

"Nothing, I'm just, I'm really proud."

Lilly stood in position on the high platforms. The music began as the first step was taken. She wore a smile the entire time, not a single thread of fear in her body. Her confidence moved her as she cartwheeled and jumped along the rope so high in the sky. She giggled as Mia pushed a bubble-blowing Milo in a wheelbarrow along the rope. Giant multi-colored bubbles floated down to the audience turning into confetti when they popped. When they got backstage Mia and Milo carried Lilly on their shoulders. She laughed as they walked around with her and cheered over-enthusiastically.

Drew had some time until he was up but he was itching to get it over with.

"Take your time, Drew," Wyatt said as he sat beside him.

"What if Asier decides not to obey me anymore."

"Then you change his mind. Just like you did before."

"What if I can't?"

"It's that exact thinking that's going to cause you to fail."

Drew sighed.

"Drew! You're up!" Barnaby called.

Wyatt followed Drew up to the opening in the curtain. "Don't forget why you're the Lion Tamer," he told him.

At that, Drew's demeanor instantly changed. Asier didn't stand a chance. Drew was the one toying with him, they went back and forth, putting the audience on edge. Everyone stood to their feet when Drew towered over the submissive beast. His shoulders relaxed and he threw the half-bitten chair to the floor.

"Thanks, Asier," he quietly told his lion.

All of Cirque stood shoulder-to-shoulder, hand-in-hand as they took their final bows. R.L. brought forward the newest performers and the crowd went nuts. Lilly couldn't help the tears that fell, Zoe wrapped her arm around her shoulders. Michael put one arm around Drew and one around Jordan, who only slightly stepped away and didn't even give him a glare.

"That was unbelievable!" Michael said as they all sat at dinner. They stuffed their faces like they hadn't eaten in years.

"It really was. I still feel like I imagined it all." Zoe shook her head.

"Man, who knew?" Jordan laughed, genuinely, wholeheartedly laughed.

"R.L. is a miracle worker that's for sure," Michael said in response. Jordan threw a crumpled up napkin at him. "If my family saw me up there, I don't know whether they would make fun or be proud," Michael paused for a second, "Yeah, they would definitely make fun."

"Because they wouldn't understand," Drew told him, knowing exactly how he felt.

"Well, you'll have to make them," R.L. said. He stood at the end of the table. "When you're finished there's something I have to show you."

R.L. led the group back to the Big Top. The giant posters slightly swayed.

"What are we doing?" Lilly asked.

"When you first arrived here you asked me how long you would be staying," R.L.'s voice was soft, "my answer was as long as it takes. The time has come."

"What?!" Drew said panicked. His heart started beating wildly.

"It is time for you to return," R.L. said. His voice was low, somber.

"No, we can't," Drew was the only one reacting. The others only wore confused looks.

"You have learned a great deal here at Cirque. You have changed, you have grown into your new identities. But what good is a change of heart, a changed life, if it doesn't spark change in other lives?" R.L. took a step closer to the group. "You must return home. You have a second chance, each of you, and you can't waste it. There are others, so many others who wear your same shoes. Others who hurt as you hurt. Among the things you take away from Cirque, I hope one of them is the fact that you are not alone. You have never been alone and you will never *ever* be alone. Cirque is never over. While you all know this now, there are still too many people who don't."

"But," Zoe's cracked voice could only get the one word out.

"It's okay," R.L. comforted. "It has been such a joy to have you here and one day we will meet again, and you will never have to leave Cirque if that's what you wish."

The teenagers then noticed that the room was filled with people, their circus family. They were embraced by their trainers, no one caring about being embarrassed by the tears being shed. Gina, Amelia—even Akili and Clyde—hugged the recruits goodbye.

The teenagers then looked at each other. They knew what each other were thinking, no one could form the words. They would most likely never see each other ever again.

"Thank you," Lilly said to her friends.

They all nodded and looked at each other, hoping their eyes could speak the words they couldn't seem to find.

R.L. gathered them close and smiled at them with tears in his eyes. "Going back will be dangerous, very dangerous. It will be scary, and difficult, and at times you will notice that your memories and lessons from Cirque will have begun to fade. That's what that mark on your arm is for."

They all looked down at their arms when they felt a tingling. In each of their tattoos small letters, *R.L.,* appeared.

The Ringleader continued, "I will always be with you. Your mark is to remind you, even when you feel there is no hope, that there is a family, an entire circus—an entire city of hope—that will all be waiting for your return."

CHAPTER 29.

WELCOME TO CIRQUE

"I just came to tell you that I'm going to Dana's house," James spoke.

"Dana, who?" Michael stood up and held onto James to balance himself.

"Dana, you know, hot Dana."

"Oh, yeah," Michael had no idea who James was talking about, "have fun."

James smirked and nodded. Michael watched as he walked off, confusion hitting him. He shook his head as he looked around the lawn filled with drunken teenagers.

"What?" His mind raced trying to put the pieces together. The last thing he remembered was a blinding light, tears in R.L.'s eyes. And now, was he home? Not only was he home but it was the night he died, the night he went to Cirque. He felt the buzz leave instantly as he remembered how he had decided to walk home on the back roads, which led to him being crushed by a car.

Was it all a dream? Was it all a drunken haze? Was Cirque real? Panic began to flood him. He needed Cirque to be real. He desperately needed it to have happened. He then remembered something. Slowly, cautiously, Michael turned up his left forearm. He shut his eyes tightly and chanted, "Please be there, please be there, please." He almost cried at the intense longing he had to see the mark on his arm.

And there it was. An acrobat hanging with both hands on the trapeze bar and *R.L.*

He laughed loudly as relief flooded him. But as the joy that it was real came to him, so did the overwhelming sadness that it was over.

"It's never over," R.L.'s words echoed. Michael knew why he was back here. This had been the night that his life ended. But now, it would be the night where his life would begin.

Lilly sat on her bathroom floor hunched over her toilet. She jolted back and her back hit the wall. She was home. She looked around the bathroom in a haze, staring at the toilet. Her cell phone buzzed with a text message from Maria, "Be there soon!"

"No way." Lilly stood up and went to her room. This was the night of the party.

Cirque filled her mind and tears fell down her cheeks. She was happy to be home, so incredibly happy, but her stomach twisted as she realized she would probably never see her four companions again.

She looked down at her arm and held her mark close to her heart.

"It's going to be different now," she said aloud.

She was going to make R.L. proud, she was going to help people, she was going to be better. Suddenly she remembered something. She ran down the stairs, faster than life, and wrapped her arms around her mother's shoulders.

"Lilly, what's wrong?" her mom spoke in bewilderment.

"I love you. So much." She squeezed tightly.

"I love you, too, sweetie." Something was different in her daughter, she could sense it. Her face seemed brighter, her voice more certain.

Lilly went back to her room and did what she knew she had to do.

"Hello?" Maria answered her phone.

"Let's not go tonight," Lilly told her urgently as she paced around her bedroom.

"What? Why not? We've been planning this forever!"

"Because I'm tired of it. I'm tired of this sick cycle we're in," Lilly said. Maria was silent. She had never heard so much feeling, so much determination in her friend's voice before.

"What do you want to do instead?" Maria asked.

"Just come over and stay the night. I wanna talk to you about something."

"Okay." The girls hung up the phone.

Lilly left out no details as she explained her struggle with food and her body to her best friend. She wanted to tell everyone how she had been before and how she was now, the night and day difference she felt inside.

Sirens echoed as Jordan sat in an alleyway. He stared at the brick wall across from him, at the dumpster and at the graffiti. *What!* Jordan stood up and frantically looked around.

"What the—" He looked at his arm. He needed reassurance. Sure enough, there was a bundle of flames reminding him who he was. Any minute now the four guys would jump him. He needed to get out of here and he knew exactly where to go.

Jordan's hand rapped on the door impatiently. Finally, a shocked Officer Blight opened it.

"Jordan?" Blight asked bewildered.

"I need your help," Jordan told him. Blight opened the door to his office wider and Jordan stepped in.

"What now? What did you do? Who's after you?" Blight asked quickly.

"No, it's nothing like that. You're right, about me needing to not be stuck, about me doing better."

"Just how drunk are you?" the officer asked. Jordan laughed and Blight nearly doubled over. He had never heard anything but negativity and obscenities come out of his mouth.

"I'm not drunk, I'm ready to be more. To do more, like you've been saying. I need your help though."

"Someone must've hit you really hard to knock this much sense into you."

"Yeah, sorta." Jordan chuckled. Blight didn't know if he'd ever get used to that.

"I'm glad though, Jordan. You're a good kid. You're capable of doin' some good."

"Yeah, I believe it, too. I believe a lot of things I didn't believe before."

"Well, come back tomorrow morning and we'll talk."

"Thanks." Jordan walked out onto the sidewalk and didn't even pay it any mind.

He was looking forward instead.

"Is it your stepfather? Are he and your mom fighting? Is he hurting you?" Mrs. Valencia fired question after question, noticing the flickers of fear and disgust that appeared in Zoe's eyes.

"No," Zoe's voice was barely above a whisper.

"Please, Zoe, I want to help you."

Zoe's eyes widened. She gripped the armrest of the chair she was sitting in.

"Zoe?" Mrs. Valencia watched as her eyes moved rapidly from side-to-side.

Zoe rubbed her tattoo as everything that had happened at Cirque came rushing back. She looked up at her guidance counselor. *Why would I be brought back to this moment?* she asked herself.

"Zoe, please. Please let me help."

She looked at her guidance counselor and knew why R.L. brought her back to this moment. This was her chance to change things, her chance to start over.

"Okay," Zoe spoke, "I'll let you help."

Some years later, Zoe would sit across from her stepfather with a phone to her ear and a sheet of glass separating them. Paul looked older, worn, the orange jumpsuit being the brightest thing in the room. His eyes were filled with shock to see her here. He hadn't seen her since the day in court when he was taken away.

"Hi," her voice was shaking. She took a deep breath and finally let go. "I forgive you."

Drew dropped the bottle of pills instantly. The sound of them crashing to the ground amplified in his ears and suddenly he was aware of everything. Anger bubbled inside of him, anger at R.L. for sending him back. *Why would he do this to me? Why would he send me back here? I don't belong here!*

Drew looked at the Lion Tamer on his arm and angrily kicked the cabinet in front of him. Tears streamed down his face and he looked at the pills that were now spilled all around him. He wanted to go back to Cirque. He wanted to be back with R.L., Wyatt, his friends, back with everyone. He reached for the pills scattered on the ground.

"No," he said aloud, startling himself.

He stood up and threw the pills in the toilet and flushed. He looked at himself in the mirror. He didn't look any different on the outside, but he knew he was a completely different person on the inside. In death, R.L. had brought Drew to life, he had brought them all to life. Drew wasn't going to choose death again.

"Ladies and gentlemen," the Ringleader came out on his unicycle joined by all the performers, "we at Cirque thank you for joining in our adventure. We hope you enjoyed yourselves and that what you have witnessed tonight leaves you truly believing this one truth—*Anything* is possible and *anyone* can do the impossible. Farewell and visit us again soon!"

The Cirque performers took their well-deserved bows. The elephants trumpeted, the horses neighed, and the lion let out a final roar.

As the Big Top emptied, there was a group who sat in a cloud of confusion and wonder. The Ringleader made his way over to his newest recruits. He smiled at the memory of Michael, Lilly, Jordan, Zoe and Drew and he knew they were going to be just fine.

"Hello, my name is R.L.," R.L. smiled as he looked over the baffled, broken teenagers. They sat still in awed silence. He smiled and spoke.

"Welcome to Cirque."

AUTHOR'S NOTE:

I wrote Cirque for all of us broken people out there. I wrote it to remind us that we are not alone, we don't have to live as a victim, we have a purpose that no one can take away from us, and there is more to life than just ourselves.

If no one has ever told you those things before, then I am honored to be the first. Please, don't forget them.

Reread this book a million times. Underline, highlight, color over your favorite parts, write your thoughts and your own story in the margins. Find your place in the circus – then help someone else find theirs too.

If you are considering suicide, if you are considering or are already self-harming, if you are being abused – or if you are the one hurting someone else – please find someone to help you begin to live the life that's waiting for you.

There are more resources than you may realize. Here are some I can offer:

National Suicide Prevention Hotline- TEXT 273Talk to 839863 suicidepreventionlifeline.org
1-800-273-8255

Youthline- TEXT teen2teen to 839863 - 877-968-8491

National Domestic Violence Hotline- 1-800-799-7233 - thehotline.org

Eating Disorder Awareness and Prevention - 1-800-931-2237 - national eating disorders.org

National Sexual Assault Hotline - 1-800-656-4637 - rainn.org

GriefShare - 1-800-395-5755 - griefshare.org

New Life Clinics - 1-800-639-5433 - newlife.com

United Way Crisis Helpline - 211 - unitedway.org

Focus on the Family - 1-855-771-4357 - focusonthefamily.com/get-help/

Alcohol & Drug Helpline- TEXT recoverynow to 839863 - 800-923-4357

Ourcirque.com - join our circus community through a free account.

The only rule of Cirque—Don't keep it for yourself. We are not alone, so we should never feel like it. Share your experience with everyone you can. This is for all of us. This is Our Cirque.

Ourcirque.com #ourcirque

CIRQUE WOULD NOT
HAVE HAPPENED WITHOUT...

Mom & Dad
Lea
Bini
Jon
Kim
Erika
Will
Shiloh
Maria
Tapestry Church
Maw Maw
Fr. Lenny
Sam
Justina
Christine
Erwin
Brogan
Brock
Madelyn
Daniella
Andy
Paw Paw
Nate
Joy
Joel
Grandma Kathy
Casey
Tara
Reese
Shannen
Stephenie
Markus
Karen
Nhena
Gally
Amy
Lizzie
Gia
Toni
Mrs. Downing
Chelsea
Mr. Tubera
Granny
Grandpa
Gi
Urban
Thread
"To Kill a Mockingbird"
"The Outsiders"
GOD
Erika
Sanny

ABOUT THE AUTHOR

Brooklynn Langston knew she wanted to be an author after reading *The Outsiders* for the first time in the sixth grade. The call to write something that would impact her generation was so loud, she couldn't hear anything else. She knew there was a story about broken people finding hope that had to be told. She began writing *Cirque* her junior year of high school (nearly failing all other classes to do so) and in 2019 decided to establish her own publishing company, Langston Publishing, to be able to finally release *Cirque* in 2020 instead of waiting around for a company to do it for her. She has worked with the youth of Jersey City as a youth pastor for several years, worked as a substitute teacher, and dreamed of the day when she'd be able to share the story of *Cirque* with the world. She currently lives in Jersey City, NJ and attends Tapestry Church. Find out more on ourcirque.com.